CONCORD CUNNINGHAM
ON THE CASE

THE

Scripture
Sleuth 3

By
Mathew Halverson

CONCORD CUNNINGHAM ON THE CASE:
THE *Scripture Sleuth 3*
Mathew Halverson

Copyright © 2003 FOCUS PUBLISHING
All rights reserved.

Cover Design by Gayle Yarrington
Cover Illustration by Don Stewart

ISBN 1-885904-39-8

PRINTED IN THE UNITED STATES OF AMERICA
by
FOCUS PUBLISHING
Bemidji, Minnesota 56601

For Lindsay

Contents

1
THE LOST
LUMBERJACK

Pine Tops residents could hardly believe it. The old lumberjack statue in the town square had been stolen. Everyone wondered where the thief had taken it. And, of course, they wondered who the thief was. But what they wondered most of all was why anyone would want to steal the old wooden statue. After all, most people considered it quite ugly. The lumberjack's body was lopsided, its legs were crooked, and its nose was strangely long and pointed.

Despite all of its faults, many long-time Pine Tops residents had become quite attached to the statue. It had stood in the town square for decades. Now that it was gone, they began to miss it. Even the birds, who loved to perch on the lumberjack's pointed nose, seemed sad that it was gone.

So, it wasn't surprising that the Cunningham house received many phone calls about the theft. Folks knew that the best hope for getting the statue back was to make sure that the best detective in Pine Tops was trying to find it. And he was. Concord Cunningham was on the case.

Concord could solve mysteries that no one else could. He didn't use fancy computer programs, special gadgets, or detective kits. He used his Bible. And his head. No matter what the mystery was, Concord could find a clue in the Bible that would help him crack the case.

The day after the lumberjack statue was stolen, Concord's dad was doing an investigation of his own. As the top reporter for the local newspaper, the *Ponderosa Press*, Mr. Cunningham was asked to cover the story. As usual, Mr. Cunningham decided to interview Pine Tops Police Chief Riggins. And, due to popular demand, Concord was invited to tag along with his dad.

"Is it true that there's a reward being offered to anyone who finds the statue?" Concord asked. He stepped into the car and placed his backpack on his lap. He seldom went anywhere without the pack.

"It's true," Mr. Cunningham answered. He fastened his seatbelt and started the car. "The city is offering one thousand dollars for the statue or information leading to the statue's recovery."

Concord raised his eyebrows in surprise. "I know the statue is old, but I didn't realize it was worth that much," the slim, sandy-haired boy said.

"No one else did either," Mr. Cunningham explained. "But people started researching the statue's history after it was stolen. It turns out that the statue was carved by one of the first lumberjacks that lived in Pine Tops. He actually carved the statue with his ax."

"I guess that's why its nose looks like a carrot," Concord said with a chuckle.

His dad chuckled, too. "Yeah, I imagine it's pretty difficult to carve a face with an ax," he agreed.

A few minutes later they had parked the car in the police station parking lot and were walking toward the station entrance. They were just a few feet from the door when Chief Riggins came bursting out.

"Hi, Chief!" Mr. Cunningham said. "Is there a crime in progress?" The tall reporter whipped out his reporter's notebook.

"Not that I know of," the chief said as he jolted to a stop. Chief Riggins was a plump man who always wore a freshly pressed uniform. "But I think a crime is about to be solved."

"Did you find the lumberjack statue?" Concord asked.

The chief nodded. "I just got a call from a man up at Bigwood Lake," he said. "He says that he and his wife found the statue. I'm on my way there to check it out." The chief gave his black moustache a few strokes as he thought for a moment. "If the statue really is there, I could use some help bringing it back. All my deputies are out on patrol. Would you two like to come along?" he asked.

"You bet!" Concord and his father said together.

The three of them hurried over to the police department truck and were soon driving to Bigwood Lake, which was just a few minutes away.

"So who found the statue, Chief?" Mr. Cunningham asked as they drove.

"Their names are Christopher and Christy Gilliam," the chief said. "Mr. Gilliam contacted the police department using the radio on his boat."

"Did they find the statue in the lake?" Concord asked.

"That's what I thought at first," the chief said. "But Mr. Gilliam said they saw the statue on a beach on the eastern shore. They're motoring across the lake to McCall's dock right now to meet us. We'll hop in their boat and they'll take us to the statue."

"And if the statue is there, the Gilliams will be a thousand dollars richer," Mr. Cunningham added.

They arrived at McCall's dock a few minutes later and jumped out of the truck. Concord scanned the lake. In the distance he saw a small motorboat approaching.

"There they are!" Concord exclaimed as he pointed.

Chief Riggins hurried out to the end of McCall's dock, and Concord and Mr. Cunningham followed. Two minutes later, the boat arrived.

"Hello, Chief!" a man shouted over the noise of the boat's motor. "I'm Christopher Gilliam." He was a tall, muscular man with short brown hair, and he was wearing just a swimsuit. "This is my wife, Christy." Mr. Gilliam handed one of the boat's ropes to his wife.

"Nice to meet you," she said as she tied the rope to a metal ring on the dock. She had brown curly hair and she also wore a swimsuit.

The chief nodded at both. Then he continued the introductions. "This is Mr. Cunningham from the *Ponderosa Press*," the chief said, "and this is his son, Concord."

Mr. Gilliam's eyes brightened when he saw Mr. Cunningham. "Are you doing a newspaper story about us finding the lumberjack statue?" he asked.

"I sure am," Mr. Cunningham said. "The whole town is anxious to know where the statue is."

"Why don't the three of you come aboard, and we'll take you there," Mr. Gilliam said.

The chief and the two Cunninghams stepped into the boat, and Mrs. Gilliam untied the rope from McCall's dock. Then she and Mr. Gilliam raised their sandy feet to the side of the dock and pushed the boat away.

"Great day to be on the beach," Mr. Cunningham said as he noticed the sand falling off their feet.

Mr. Gilliam nodded. "And it's a great day to get a one thousand dollar reward!" he said excitedly. Then he fired up the engine, turned the boat toward the eastern shore of the lake, and throttled up.

They zoomed across the lake. The noise of the motor and the wind made it difficult to talk, so everyone decided to wait to discuss the discovery until they stopped.

About ten minutes later they arrived at a remote beach on the eastern side of the lake. Mr. Gilliam steered the boat to a small floating dock. The dock extended about fifteen feet into the water from the beach. As Mrs. Gilliam began tying the rope to the dock, Mr. Gilliam pointed to the beach. "There's the lumberjack!" he announced.

The statue was standing at the back edge of the beach. It was in the shadows of the trees behind it, so it was a little difficult to see. The group began stepping from the boat to the dock, one person at a time.

"There aren't any roads to this side of the lake," Mr. Cunningham said as he stepped out.

"The thief probably used a boat to get the statue here," Chief Riggins said as he stepped onto the dock.

Mr. Cunningham nodded in agreement and scribbled a few notes. The rest of the group made it out of the boat, and they all walked up the dock to the beach. They stepped off the dock into the sand and made their way toward the lumberjack. About halfway across the beach, the group stopped. Chief Riggins asked them to wait there while he made certain the area was safe.

It didn't take long for him to confirm that the statue was there by itself, and the thief was long gone. Chief Riggins then motioned everyone over, and the group approached the statue.

"Yep, this is it!" Chief Riggins declared.

Mr. Cunningham looked at the statue and nodded with a chuckle. "I think we'd all recognize that lumberjack anywhere," he said, agreeing the statue wasn't a fake. Then he turned to Mr. Gilliam. "So did you find the statue just a short while ago?" he asked.

"About thirty minutes ago," Mr. Gilliam said. "We had been cruising around the lake for a while and we were starting to get hot. So, we anchored the boat about one hundred feet off the shore of this beach and jumped into the water to cool off. While we were swimming around our boat we saw somebody staring at us from the beach. The person kept staring and staring, and we couldn't tell who he was since we were so far out in the lake. So, we climbed back into the boat and grabbed the binoculars. I focused on the guy and saw that it was the lumberjack statue!"

"Did you come over to the statue after you saw it through the binoculars?" Mr. Cunningham asked.

"Nope," Mr. Gilliam said. "We decided to just radio the police. We didn't know if the thief was still around, and he might be a dangerous guy. After we radioed the police, we pulled up our anchor, fired up the motor, and went straight to McCall's dock to meet Chief Riggins."

Concord dropped his backpack to the ground and pulled out his Bible. Something about the Gilliams' story was bothering him. He sat on a log and flipped to the concordance section of his Bible. Then he began looking up verses.

"Did you see anyone else around?" the chief asked, hoping for a description of the thief.

"Nope," Mr. Gilliam said. "There was no one around. That's why we decided to go swimming here. We had this part of the lake all to ourselves."

Mr. Cunningham scribbled one more note and closed his notebook. "Well, Chief," he said, "it looks like the town of Pine Tops owes the Gilliams one thousand dollars for finding the statue."

Concord suddenly looked up from his Bible with his finger on a verse. "I'm not so sure about that, Dad," he said.

Mr. Gilliam nervously bit his lower lip. "What are you talking about?" he asked. "We found the statue. We told you exactly what happened."

"Actually, you didn't," Concord said. "Your story can't be true."

"What makes you say that?" Mr. Gilliam asked.

"John 13:5," Concord said as he held out his Bible. "There's something you forgot."

How did Concord know that the Gilliams were lying?

Read John 13:5 for the clue that Concord gave the group.

The solution to *"The Lost Lumberjack"* is on page 88.

2
PINE TEA

The Cunningham house was usually one of the busiest houses on Lodgepole Lane. With three active kids, Mr. Cunningham's endless reporting assignments, and Mrs. Cunningham's volunteer activities, there was always somebody coming or going. But every now and then the family managed to sit down together on the front porch and enjoy a large glass of Mrs. Cunningham's delicious lemonade.

"Outstanding lemonade, dear," Mr. Cunningham said after a large gulp. "I don't know how you do it."

"Yeah, Mom," Concord's older brother, Cody, agreed. Cody was a few inches taller than Concord and had short curly hair. "This lemonade is outta sight! Do you have some kind of secret ingredient in there?"

"Maybe," Mrs. Cunningham replied. Her long brown hair swayed as she rocked in her chair and smirked.

Before Cody could pry for more information, Concord's spunky younger sister, Charlotte, suddenly tapped Concord on the arm. "Hey Concord," she said, "do you want to play the front porch guessing game?"

Concord took a drink as he considered the offer.

"I'll play," Cody said while Concord's glass was still at his lips.

"I'll play, too," Mrs. Cunningham said.

"Why don't we all play," Mr. Cunningham added.

Concord finally finished the drink. "Wow, a lot can happen while a guy takes a drink of lemonade," he joked. Everyone chuckled. "Sure, I'd love to play, too," he added.

The game was simple. Each person would guess what kind of vehicle would drive past the Cunningham house next. A person could guess car, truck, or motorcycle. But if the guess was a car, the player also had to guess a color. Most of the vehicles that drove by were cars, so that was a way to keep the game fair.

"I'll guess a red car," said Charlotte.

"Put me down for a truck," said Cody.

"Hmm," Mrs. Cunningham said as she thought about her guess. "I'll try a yellow car."

"Better put me down for a motorcycle," Mr. Cunningham guessed.

Concord scratched his cheek as he thought of a guess. "I'll try a blue car," he finally said.

The guesses were all made, and now all the players could do was wait to see what came down Lodgepole Lane next.

A moment later, Cody said, "I think I hear one coming!" The Cunninghams all scooted forward to the edges of their seats and stared at the corner about three houses down.

"I hear it, too," Concord agreed, "but it doesn't sound like a car."

"And it doesn't sound like a motorcycle," Mr. Cunningham said with a shrug.

"Yeah," Charlotte said, "it sounds more like a—"

Everyone gasped. Turning around the corner and onto Lodgepole Lane were two horses!

"Wow!" Charlotte exclaimed as she bounced in excitement. "There are horses on our street!"

"I guess we'll need a new category for the front porch game," Concord joked as everyone stared at the horses.

There was a man on each horse. Both riders seemed to be dressed for the woods. They wore blue jeans, flannel shirts, scruffy hats, and boots. There were also large packs hung over the back of each horse, just behind the saddles.

The two riders were discussing something. One rider pulled a piece of paper out of his pocket and they both looked at it. The other rider then pointed at the Cunningham house. A few strides later, both riders pulled on their reigns and said, "Whoa!" The horses stopped.

"Good evening, folks!" one rider called out to the Cunninghams. "My name's Rusty, and this is my trail partner, Lefty." Both men tipped their hats. "We were wonderin' if this might be where The Concordance lives?"

"It sure is!" Cody exclaimed. "Here he is!" Cody reached over and slapped Concord on the back. Concord gave a nervous wave.

"The Concordance" was a nickname given to Concord by Chief Riggins after Concord had solved his first mystery. The nickname was quite fitting. Concord was an ace with the concordance at the back of his Bible. He used it to look up verses about ideas, words, and people in the Bible. The verses he found helped him answer questions and solve mysteries.

"Mr. Concordance," Rusty said, "would you be willing to help me solve a little mystery?"

Concord looked over at his dad. Mr. Cunningham nodded, which meant it was okay.

"I'll try," Concord said to Rusty.

"Well that's mighty neighborly of ya," Rusty said. Rusty and Lefty dismounted their horses and tied them to a tree in the Cunninghams' front yard. Then they sauntered over to the porch. "We work as trail guides up on Mount Redhead," Rusty continued. "We've been hearin' about Mr. Concord Cunningham solving all sorts of mysteries down here in Pine Tops. When I couldn't figure out my mystery, I thought that Lefty and I could come into town and see if you could solve it. If you can, I'd like to treat your whole family to a free trail ride on Mount Redhead."

The Cunninghams all smiled and looked at each other in excitement. Mount Redhead was a towering mountain that could be seen from just about anywhere in Pine Tops. Thick pine trees and vegetation covered much of the mountain, and above the tree line were steep granite slopes and cliffs. The mountain was capped with a patch of dark red rocks, giving Mount Redhead its name.

"You see, we had a couple of free days between jobs, so Lefty and I were exploring a little-known trail on the southern side of Mount Redhead," Rusty said. "We were about halfway through our day when I looked up the trail about thirty yards and saw a Schwandt Pine."

"A what?" Concord asked.

"A Schwandt Pine. It's a very rare species of pine tree, so you hardly ever see one," Rusty said. "But any trail rider knows that the Schwandt Pine is the best pine tree for one thing in particular."

"What's that?" Concord asked.

"Good tea," Lefty mumbled, speaking for the first time.

"Right, Lefty," Rusty said.

"I thought tea was made out of leaves," Charlotte said.

"Usually that's true, little Miss," Rusty replied. "But a lot of us trail riders have been making pine tea for years. It's quick, easy, and you never run out of pine needles in the woods."

"So you use pine needles instead of tea bags?" Concord asked.

"That's right," Rusty said. "Anyway, we decided to cut a branch off that Schwandt Pine and take it with us.

We wanted to use some of its needles to make tea that night. We rode four or five more hours, and then we decided to stop for the night. We set up camp and started a fire. Once the fire was going, we plucked all the needles off the Schwandt Pine branch and threw them into our kettle. Then we filled the kettle with water all the way to the top. We wanted to make plenty because we knew that those Schwandt Pine needles make such—"

"Good tea," Lefty mumbled again.

"Right, Lefty," Rusty said. "We put the kettle on a rock on the edge of the fire and waited for it to heat up. About half an hour later, it was ready. So, I poured tea into our two cups and put the kettle back on its rock. We put a spoonful of sugar in each cup, leaned back against a log, and enjoyed the tea."

"Nothing sounds too mysterious there," Concord said. "Except that you can actually make tea from pine needles."

The group chuckled.

"Well," Rusty replied. "There's more. As I drank my cup of tea, I became more and more tired. As soon as I got to the bottom of the cup, I fell asleep! I slept like a baby all night. When I woke up in the morning, I figured I could have another cup of tea for breakfast. After all, we made a whole kettle. But when I went over to the kettle, it was empty!"

"It sounds like Lefty had quite a few cups of tea," Mr. Cunningham said. Lefty scowled at Mr. Cunningham.

"That's what I thought," Rusty said. "I told Lefty that he owed me half a kettle of Schwandt Pine tea. But he said that's impossible. Lefty says that he only had one cup of tea and then fell asleep for the night, too."

"So the mystery is what happened to the rest of the tea?" Concord asked.

"That's right," Rusty said with a nod. "Of course, if you ask Lefty, it's no mystery at all. He says that the rest of the tea steamed off during the night. You see, we never moved the kettle off that rock on the edge of the fire. Lefty says that the tea eventually steamed away just like if you leave a pan of water on a hot stove."

Concord considered the possibility. Then he asked, "Could we see your kettle?"

"Sure thing," Rusty said. He walked over to his horse and untied a flap on one of the bags hanging over the horse's back. He pulled out a black metal kettle and walked back to the porch. He handed it to Concord.

Concord studied it for a minute and then turned to his mom. "Mom, how much water do you think this kettle holds?"

Mrs. Cunningham looked at the kettle. "It's pretty large," she said. "I'd say it probably holds about a gallon."

"Do you think that much water could steam off in a night?" Concord asked.

She thought for a moment. "I think it would be close," she said. "I don't know if it would all steam off in a night or not."

The group was silent for a moment.

"What if a deer or something came and drank the tea?" Charlotte asked. "You were both asleep after the first cup, so maybe an animal decided to have a drink."

"Or maybe even another hiker or trail guide," Cody added.

"Those are good ideas, kids," Rusty nodded. "I thought of all that, too. But we checked the dirt around the kettle and there were no tracks except our own." Rusty rubbed his chin and looked at Concord. "So what do you think?" he asked. "Does Lefty owe me half a kettle of Schwandt Pine tea or not?"

Concord stood up and walked into the house.

"Where's he going?" asked Rusty. "Is he giving up?"

"I don't think so," Mr. Cunningham said, knowing that his son was going to get a Bible. "He's just getting started."

A few moments later Concord walked back onto the porch with an open Bible.

"Rusty," Concord said, "Lefty does owe you half a kettle of Schwandt Pine tea."

"Huh?" Lefty grunted in surprise.

Rusty's eyebrows shot up. "I knew it!" he exclaimed. "But how do you know?"

"Here," The Concordance said with a smile as he handed Rusty the Bible. "Read Proverbs 26:20 and see if you can figure it out, too."

How did Concord know that Lefty drank the tea?

Read Proverbs 26:20 for the clue that Concord gave Rusty.

The solution to *"Pine Tea"* is on page 89.

3
THE FACE SCRIBBLER

During lunchtime, Concord's schoolyard was one of the most secure places in town. It didn't have a tall fence or a strong gate, but it did have a tall man with a strong scowl watching the students. Principal Ironsides was on patrol.

After being called out of his office many times over the years to investigate lunchtime problems, he finally decided to spend the lunch hour outside. It seemed to work. Whenever students saw him, they settled down and became perfectly behaved. Even the Burley twins stopped their lunchtime scams when Principal Ironsides was patrolling. After all, nobody wanted to be dragged back to the principal's office and given a punishment, which was usually some kind of disgusting cleaning job.

Principal Ironsides had a sharp eye and was able to continuously scan most of the schoolyard. In fact, he was often at trouble spots almost before the trouble began. As a result, quite a few students would follow him around each day, curious to see what kind of troublemakers he would catch. Principal Ironsides didn't necessarily enjoy the followers, but sometimes they came in handy.

"Go find Cunningham!" Principal Ironsides barked one day to one of the students following him. The boy sprinted towards a large Ponderosa Pine on the edge of the field. Concord was often near the tree with a friend.

"Concord!" the runner yelled while he was still halfway across the field. Concord and his friend Charlie Lowman looked up and saw the boy coming.

"Somebody's sure in a hurry to see you," said Charlie, who often joined Concord under the tree.

A few moments later, the runner was standing in front of them and trying to catch his breath.

"Concord," the runner said between quick breaths. "Mr. Ironsides wants you to come over to the big boulder."

"Did he tell you why?" Concord asked as he stood and slung his backpack over his shoulder.

"It's two boys," the runner said. "One of them did something wrong and Principal Ironsides can't figure out which one."

"It sounds like Mr. Ironsides needs The Concordance to crack the case!" Charlie said. His messy hair bounced as he sprang to his feet.

"Let's go!" Concord exclaimed, and the three boys hurried toward Principal Ironsides.

After a quick jog across the field, the boys arrived at the big boulder. The boulder was a huge piece of granite about seven feet tall and ten feet wide. Some students enjoyed resting on the big boulder or leaning against it during the lunch hour.

As Concord tried to catch his breath, he observed the scene. Next to the boulder was a crowd of kids surrounding Principal Ironsides, who was talking to two boys. Concord immediately recognized the two boys. John Spencer and Robbie Lockey were two friends who expressed their friendship in a strange way; they were always trying get each other into trouble.

"Aren't those the two guys who set off the smoke bomb in the bathroom a while ago," Charlie said quietly to Concord.

"Yeah," Concord whispered back. "Actually one of them did it and tried to blame it on the oth-" Concord suddenly stopped as he saw the reason he had been called over by Principal Ironsides. John had blue ink all over his face. And it wasn't just a little ink. Somebody had scribbled on his cheeks, chin, forehead, and nose.

"Whoa," Charlie said as he saw John's face. "It looks like somebody's been drawing on John's face, except they forgot to actually make a picture," he remarked.

Principal Ironsides suddenly noticed that Concord had arrived. "Cunningham!" he barked. Principal Ironside's tone of voice always made Concord feel like he was in the Army.

Concord was tempted to salute, but he restrained himself. "Hello, Mr. Ironsides," he said as his back straightened.

"You've probably noticed that we've got a situation here," Principal Ironsides said. He turned toward John. John had thick black hair and wore brown-rimmed glasses. Mr. Ironsides shook his head as he looked at John. "John's face seems to have had an unpleasant encounter with a pen."

The crowd of students laughed.

"Quiet!" Principal Ironsides roared. The students were immediately silent. "Okay Cunningham, John says that Robbie Lockey did this to him." Concord glanced to the right and saw Robbie, tall and blond, shaking his head.

"No way," Robbie said. "I didn't do this. John's making it all up to get me into trouble."

"Do you think I would do this to myself?" John asked as he pointed to his face.

"You must have," Robbie said, "because it sure wasn't me."

Principal Ironsides held up his hands to stop the argument. Then he turned back to Concord. "These two can't seem to carry on a conversation without arguing," he said with disgust. "Here's the deal. I saw John come out of the cafeteria and lie down by the big boulder. A few minutes later, Robbie came over to John for a moment and then left. Robbie had his back to me, so I don't know if he wrote on John's face or not. Now, I'm going to have each boy tell us his side of the story, and I want you to tell me who's telling the truth and who's lying."

Concord swallowed hard and gave a small nod.

"John, you go first," Principal Ironsides said as he put his hands on his hips.

"Okay," John replied as he pushed his glasses up his nose. "It's real simple. I didn't sleep well last night so I decided to relax next to the big boulder today during lunch. I was so tired that I actually fell asleep for a few minutes. When I woke up, I discovered that somebody had drawn all over my face. I saw Robbie walking away with a pen in his hand, so I knew it was him. That's when I started yelling for Mr. Ironsides."

Robbie's lips tightened in frustration. Principal Ironsides turned to him. "Your turn, Robbie."

"What John said isn't true," he said angrily. "Here's what really happened. I was eating my lunch in the cafeteria. John came over to me and asked if I would visit him by the big boulder when I was finished eating. I said I would. I went out to the boulder when I was finished, but John was sleeping so I walked away."

Principal Ironsides turned back to Concord. "Well, Cunningham, there isn't much to go on here. What do you think?"

The crowd stared at Concord. He scratched his cheek as he thought. "Could I ask a couple questions?" he asked.

"Be my guest," said Principal Ironsides. Then he turned to John and Robbie. "And if you boys don't cooperate, you'll both be cleaning the locker rooms after school for two weeks. Got it?"

Both boys nodded.

Concord considered asking each boy if he had a blue pen, but he knew that wouldn't really prove anything. Each boy could have thrown the pen away or might even have a blue pen that wasn't the one that drew on John's face.

Concord turned to John. "Is it possible that somebody instead of Robbie drew on your face?" he asked.

"I don't think so," John said. "He was the only one I saw walking away when I woke up. Nobody else was even close to me until Mr. Ironsides came over."

"John's right," Principal Ironsides agreed. "I always keep a close eye on the big boulder at lunch. The only two people who have been near it today are John and Robbie."

Concord nodded and continued.

"John, wouldn't you wake up if Robbie was drawing on your face?" Concord asked.

"Well, I didn't," John said. "I would have stopped him if I had."

Concord nodded again. "Is there any ink on your hands?" Concord asked.

John smiled. "Nope," he replied. He proudly held out his clean hands. "But there might have been if I had been drawing on my own face. Pens are messy, you know." Concord decided that wasn't always true. He had written many things without smudging ink on his fingers.

"One more question," Concord said. "John, did you have a coat or backpack with you out here?"

"Nope," John said. "I ate my lunch in the cafeteria and came straight out here to the big boulder with nothing."

Concord turned to Principal Ironsides. "I've got your answer for you, Mr. Ironsides."

"What?" Principal Ironsides exclaimed. "Don't you need to ask Robbie any questions? How do you know which one of these boys is lying?"

Concord dropped his backpack to the ground and pulled out his Bible. He opened to the book of James and pointed to a verse.

"There's a clue right here in James 1:23," The Concordance said. "John must be lying. He scribbled on his own face so he could blame Robbie."

How did Concord know that John made up the story about Robbie?

Read James 1:23 for the clue that Concord gave Principal Ironsides.

The solution to *"The Face Scribbler"* is on page 90.

4
REDHEAD ROSES

"What's going on?" Concord asked his mom as they drove past the Pine Tops Flower Shop.

"Good question," Mrs. Cunningham replied. There was a large crowd in front of the shop, including a news van from the local radio station, KONE-FM. "Maybe it's a clearance sale," she said. "You know, our house could use a few flowers. I think we should stop and—"

"Smell the roses?" Concord interrupted. He flashed a grin at his mom.

"Very funny," she said with a chuckle as she pulled into a nearby parking lot. "I was going to say we should stop to see if there are any good deals. But it never hurts to smell a rose or two." Then something caught her eye. She raised her eyebrows and then added, "Especially if it's a Redhead Rose." She pointed to a sign, which simply said REDHEAD ROSES.

"A Redhead Rose?" Concord repeated curiously.

"You've never heard about Redhead Roses?" she asked with surprise. "They're the most famous flower around."

"I guess I've never paid much attention to flowers," Concord replied.

"The Redhead Rose is a special species," Mrs. Cunningham explained. "It's a wild rose that's only found in one place: near the top of the tree line on Mount Redhead."

"Do you mean that Redhead Roses don't grow any-where else?" Concord asked.

"That's right," Mrs. Cunningham said. "Local garden-ers have been trying to grow them in yards and gardens for years, but no one's been able to do it. They think that the soil on Mount Redhead must be special somehow. So, they've tried different mixes of soil and fertilizer, but nothing's worked."

"Are Redhead Roses prettier than regular roses?" Concord asked.

"Some people think so," Mrs. Cunningham replied. "But what really makes them unique is their scent. They smell like a cross between a fresh red rose and a sweet pine tree. There's really nothing like it. They only last for a couple days and then they wilt, so you really have to enjoy them while you have them."

"If people like them so much and they only grow on Mount Redhead, Redhead Roses must be expensive," Concord reasoned.

"Oh yes," Mrs. Cunningham said. "They're always the most expensive flower in the shop. They never go on sale, either. So, if this is some kind of special deal, I'm going to buy a few for sure. It's been years since we've had a Redhead Rose in our house."

Concord and his mom quickly walked from the park-ing lot to the front of the Pine Tops Flower Shop and tried to find a spot where they could see through the crowd. Though they had trouble seeing, hearing was no problem at all. KONE-FM was doing a live broadcast from the front of the shop, and there were large speakers set up so everyone could hear what was going over the air.

The radio announcer with long brown hair and a flan-nel shirt was standing before the crowd. Just as a song was ending, he held a microphone up to his mouth and began speaking. The crowd quieted to listen.

"Good afternoon to all of you listening at home and all of you here with me," he said. "I'm Woody Jones broadcasting this special report live from the Pine Tops Flower Shop. We've got quite the crowd growing here." Woody turned to a short man with gray hair standing next to him. "I'm standing next to Bruce Oliver, the owner of the Pine Tops Flower Shop. Mr. Oliver, it looks like the word is already out about your big breakthrough."

"Yes," Mr. Oliver said. "I guess everyone is as excited as we are."

"For those people who haven't yet heard the news," Woody began, "let us bring you up to speed on a story that KONE-FM first broke one hour ago. The Pine Tops Flower Shop announced today that it has figured out a way to grow Redhead Roses right here in the town of Pine Tops!"

Mrs. Cunningham's eyes bulged. "I can't believe it," she whispered to Concord. There were gasps throughout the crowd from people who were hearing the news for the first time.

"I wonder how they did it?" Concord whispered back. They both turned their attention to the front of the crowd as Woody continued the interview with Mr. Oliver.

"Mr. Oliver, this discovery took a lot of research, didn't it?" Woody asked.

"It sure did," Mr. Oliver replied. "The first thing our shop did was analyze the soil near the top of Mount Redhead's tree line."

"You did that because Mount Redhead's tree line is the only place where Redhead Roses are known to grow, right?" Woody asked.

"Right," Mr. Oliver confirmed. "But we couldn't find anything unusual about the soil there."

"So, Mr. Oliver," Woody continued, "what did you do then?"

"Well, we decided that Mount Redhead's soil must not be the special condition that Redhead Roses need to grow," Mr. Oliver explained. "We decided it was the air."

"Is that because there's no pollution on Mount Redhead such as there might be around a town?" Woody asked.

"Not exactly," Mr. Oliver said. "It wasn't the air quality we looked at, it was the air pressure."

Concord looked at his mom. She raised an eyebrow in interest.

"For those of us who don't really know much about air pressure, could you explain what you mean?" Woody asked.

"Sure. There's less and less air pressure the higher you go," Mr. Oliver explained. "Basically, the higher you are, the less air there is above you, so the pressure coming down on you is less. Therefore, the air pressure up at the tree line on Mount Redhead is much less than it is down here in Pine Tops."

The crowd murmured in excitement as everyone began to understand the explanation.

Concord looked over at his mom. "Makes sense," Mrs. Cunningham whispered.

"So how did you change the air pressure in Pine Tops so that the Redhead Roses would grow down here?" Woody asked.

"Obviously we couldn't change the air pressure of the whole town," Mr. Oliver said. "But we could change the air pressure in this." He turned to his right and pointed to something. Concord and his mom couldn't see, so they quickly shuffled to find a better spot. They worked their way around the back of the crowd to the far side of the shop where there were more gaps between onlookers.

They could now see that Mr. Oliver was pointing to a big glass case with some kind of air compressor on top, a car battery on the side, and a Redhead Rose bush inside of it.

"We call it the Redhead Rose Machine," Mr. Oliver said. "This case was sealed shut at the tree line of Mount Redhead, and the air compressor keeps the air pressure the same as it was when the box was sealed."

"So the rose bush is growing in what seems to be the same altitude as the tree line of Mount Redhead?" Woody asked.

"Right," Mr. Oliver confirmed. "The air compressor on top of the box also blows in fresh air, just as the plant would receive on Mount Redhead. It sucks just enough old air out to maintain the correct pressure."

Concord turned to his mom. "Would all that work, Mom?" he asked.

"It should," she said. "If the box is airtight, the compressor should be able to maintain whatever air pressure it's set to maintain."

Woody pointed to the car battery. "And why did you use a car battery to power the compressor instead of electricity?" he asked.

"We did that so the machine could be moved around," Mr. Oliver explained. "When the machine gets to a permanent spot, it can be plugged into an outlet with the cord on the back." He reached behind the machine and held up a cord. "When plugged in, the air compressor will instantly switch from battery power to electricity. So, it won't miss a beat and the plant will never feel a difference in air pressure."

"Folks," Woody said, "I know that many of you have dug up Redhead Rose bushes on Mount Redhead and tried to plant them in your yard here in Pine Tops. And what always happens within a couple days?"

"They wilt!" several people yelled from the audience.

"That's right," Woody agreed. "They wilt terribly and they look awful. But look at this Redhead Rose bush. It looks fantastic! Mr. Oliver, how long has this bush been down from the mountain?"

"Five days," Mr. Oliver proudly announced. The crowd applauded.

Concord looked carefully at the bush. As far as he could tell, it was in excellent condition. "Looks pretty good to me," he said to his mom.

"It really does look healthy," Mrs. Cunningham agreed.

Woody raised his hand to stop the applause. "Folks, believe it or not, it gets even better," he said. "Mr. Oliver, why don't you tell us what your store is offering to the fine people of Pine Tops."

"We thought that there might be some folks who would be interested in having a Redhead Rose Machine of their own," Mr. Oliver said. Most of the crowd applauded and a few people even gave loud whistles. "So, we built one hundred Redhead Rose Machines!" As the crowd applauded again, Mr. Oliver turned toward a huge truck parked in the alley next to the shop. "Larry, bring 'em on out!" he shouted.

A large, muscular man started carrying the sealed glass boxes from the back of the truck to the front of the store. Inside each box was a layer of dirt and a medium sized bush planted in the middle. Each plant was green and healthy, but none had a rose yet.

"Now folks," Mr. Oliver said, "Our store is selling these Redhead Rose Machines on a first come, first served basis." Some folks began forming a line at the shop's door. "Each machine was sealed at the tree line of Mount

Redhead and the air compressors are all maintaining the correct pressure and pumping in fresh air."

"And Mr. Oliver, why don't any of these bushes have roses on them yet?" Woody asked.

"Basically," Mr. Oliver said, "we didn't think it would be fair to the rest of Pine Tops to dig up all the Redhead Rose bushes that were blooming on the mountain. Instead, we dug up some of the bushes that haven't yet bloomed. But they will bloom soon."

"Hmm," Mrs. Cunningham sighed. "I'd love to get one of these machines if this is for real, and they aren't too expensive. So, Mr. Concordance, what do you think? Should I go get in line?"

Concord decided to accept the challenge and investigate the situation. He dropped his backpack to the ground and pulled out his Bible. As he flipped through the pages of the concordance section, Woody asked Mr. Oliver another question.

"Mr. Oliver," Woody said, "how long will it take for these bushes in the machines to produce Redhead Roses?"

"We think each plant is about two months away from producing Redhead Roses," Mr. Oliver answered. "And as soon as they bloom you can open the machine and enjoy your roses for those precious few days before they wilt."

"And what if somebody buys a machine and their Redhead Rose bush never blooms?" Woody asked.

"If the bush never blooms, we'd be happy to refund the buyer's money," Mr. Oliver said. "Just remember, plug in your machine before the battery dies. And most importantly, whatever you do, don't break the seal on the Redhead Rose Machine until you're ready to clip your roses. If you do, the correct air pressure will escape, and the Redhead Rose bush will quickly wilt as usual."

Mrs. Cunningham looked at the line in front of the store. "What do you think, Concord?" she asked. "That line is getting longer by the second."

Concord suddenly thumped a page on his Bible. "Got it!" he exclaimed. He turned to his mom. "I wouldn't buy the Redhead Rose Machine if I were you. It won't work."

"What do you mean?" his mother asked. "The roses in his first machine look great to me."

"Those do, but Mr. Oliver should have read 1 Corinthians 3:6," The Concordance said. "He's going to be giving out a lot of refunds."

How did Concord know that the Redhead Rose Machines wouldn't work?

Read 1 Corinthians 3:6 for the clue that Concord gave his mom.

The solution to *"Redhead Roses"* is on page 91.

5
DOCTORS AND DETECTIVES

"Dad, do I really need to get a physical exam?" Concord asked as the Cunninghams' car turned into the doctor's office parking lot.

"You need one if you want to play soccer this year," Mr. Cunningham replied. "It's part of the rules. Every player must get a physical exam to make sure he or she is fit to play."

Concord sighed. He disliked getting physical exams just as much as he loved playing soccer. "Maybe Dr. Steel will be sick today," he said.

Mr. Cunningham considered the thought. "If he is, he'd better have a note from his doctor," he said with a wink.

They laughed as they got out of the car and walked into the doctor's office. A few minutes later, a nurse called Concord and his dad back to an examination room.

"Dr. Steel will be with you in just a minute," the nurse said as she backed out of the room and closed the door.

"No hurry," Concord murmured, sitting down on the examination table. He wiped a drop of sweat off his forehead.

"Don't worry, Concord," Mr. Cunningham said, "Dr. Steel is a great doctor."

"It's not Dr. Steel I'm worried about," Concord explained. "It's that huge popsicle stick he pushes down my throat." It was just last year that Dr. Steel had held the tongue depressor in Concord's throat a second too long. Concord had thrown up all over him.

"I'm sure Dr. Steel has forgotten all about last year," Mr. Cunningham said. "It probably happens all the time."

"Really?" Concord said, perking up. "He must go through a lot of doctor's coats," he joked.

Before Mr. Cunningham could reply, the door opened and in walked Dr. Steel. He was a tall bald man wearing a black tie and a snow white doctor's coat.

"Good morning, Cunninghams!" Dr. Steel bellowed with a smile. He shook their hands and immediately sat down on a stool next to Concord. He glanced down at his clipboard. "So are you getting ready for another superb soccer season?" Dr. Steel asked Concord.

"Another season, yes," Concord replied. "But we'll see if it's superb."

"Well, let's look you over and see if you're ready to go," Dr. Steel said. He plucked a tongue depressor off a nearby table.

Concord took a deep breath, opened his mouth, and closed his eyes. He knew that if he could just make it through the next ten seconds the rest of the examination would be easy. Dr. Steel inserted the tongue depressor into Concord's mouth and was just about to press down on Concord's tongue when suddenly, a high-pitched ring echoed through the room.

"Hmm," Dr. Steel said as he removed the tongue depressor from Concord's mouth. He patted his coat pockets. Then he reached into his left pocket and pulled out a cell phone. "It looks like I forgot to take my cell phone out of my pocket when I came into the office this morning. I'm very sorry for the interruption."

"No problem!" Concord blurted. He took a quick breath and temporarily relaxed.

Dr. Steel answered the phone in a calm, low voice, "This is Dr. Steel." A second later he raised an eyebrow with interest. "Hello, Chief Riggins."

Concord and his dad exchanged curious looks.

Dr. Steel listened for a moment and then said, "I see. Hmm. That's an unusual request, but I think I should be able to do it." While Dr. Steel listened, Mr. Cunningham reached into his pocket for his reporter's notebook. Over the years, Mr. Cunningham had developed a keen sense for smelling a front page story. "I understand," Dr. Steel said. "I'll be there right away." He put the phone back in his pocket and turned to the Cunninghams.

"I know this is a big favor to ask, but would it be possible to reschedule this appointment?" Dr. Steel asked.

"It's very possible, as long as you tell us what's going on," Mr. Cunningham said with a friendly smile, holding his pen to his notebook.

"Chief Riggins wants me to come down to the Pine Tops Coin Shop," Dr. Steel said. "He thinks they just caught a robber there, but they need a doctor to help prove it."

A curious look spread across Mr. Cunningham's face. He excitedly began scribbling notes. Then Mr. Cunningham looked to Concord. "I don't think Concord would mind changing his appointment, would you Concord?"

"No way!" Concord replied. Then he added, "Especially if I can come with you to report this story."

Mr. Cunningham grinned. "You got it," he said. Then he turned to Dr. Steel. "I guess we'll see you there, Dr. Steel." The three of them immediately left the examination room and hurried out to their cars.

After a quick drive across town, Mr. Cunningham located a parking spot just two shops down from the Pine Tops Coin Shop. The coin shop had been in downtown Pine Tops as long as anyone could remember. It had also been robbed more times that anyone could count. It was known by thieves as the easiest burglary target in town. In fact, the old owner had become so tired of being robbed that he decided to sell the shop a few months ago.

"I wonder why the police need a doctor?" Concord asked as he grabbed his backpack out of the backseat.

"I'm not sure," Mr. Cunningham replied. "Hopefully no one was hurt."

They jumped out of the car and hurried down the sidewalk to the yellow police tape surrounding the coin shop. A moment later, Mr. Cunningham and his press pass caught Police Chief Riggins' eye. The chief motioned for Mr. Cunningham and Concord to come through the tape.

"You've been hearing about our latest crime scenes faster and faster, Mr. Cunningham," the chief said. Then he shot a wink at Concord.

"Sometimes we're just lucky," Mr. Cunningham replied with a grin. "We were with Dr. Steel when you called."

The chief chuckled at the coincidence. Then he stroked his perfectly trimmed moustache. "Where is Dr. Steel?" he asked.

"Right here!" Dr. Steel shouted as he ducked under the police tape.

"Good," Chief Riggins said. "Now, maybe we can get to the bottom of this."

Mr. Cunningham pulled out his reporter's notebook and followed Chief Riggins and Dr. Steel into the coin shop. Concord was close behind.

Inside, Concord watched several police detectives examining all the shop's windows and doors.

Mr. Cunningham scratched his cheek with his pen as he surveyed the shop. "I don't remember those bars being on the shop's windows and doors," he said.

"That's because they're not usually there," Chief Riggins replied. "The new owner put in a fancy security system right after he bought the coin shop. He knew how often the shop had been robbed in the past."

"So he thought the bars would keep the robbers out?" Concord asked.

"Actually, he thought the bars would keep the robbers in," the chief said with a smirk.

"I don't follow you, Chief," Mr. Cunningham said.

"This security system is designed to trap the thief," Chief Riggins explained. "If somebody breaks into the shop, the system waits thirty seconds and then slams bars down across the windows and doors. The thief is trapped until the police get here."

"The robber can get in, but he can't get out," Mr. Cunningham said as he scribbled a few notes.

"Exactly," the chief said.

"Did it work?" Concord asked.

"It looks like it did," Chief Riggins said with an uncertain smile. "The alarm went off early this morning, and when my deputies arrived a few minutes later there was a man trapped inside the shop."

"So why am I here, Chief?" Dr. Steel asked.

"There's one piece of the puzzle that doesn't fit," Chief Riggins replied, "We're not completely certain we have the right guy."

"How could that be?" Mr. Cunningham asked.

"Come over here," the chief said to the group, walking towards the shop's back door. He pointed to a small patch of blood on the latch. "This is why we need you, Dr. Steel. How long would you say this blood has been here?"

Dr. Steel studied the spot for a moment. Then he pulled a tissue out of his pocket and rubbed the blood. "I'd say two hours, maybe three at the most," he said.

The chief sighed. "That's what I was afraid of," he said.

"What's the problem, Chief?" Mr. Cunningham asked. "The robber cut himself when he was trying to break out of the shop, right?"

"That's what we thought," the chief said. "But the man we caught, Mr. Lang, doesn't have a scratch on him that we could find. In fact, he claims he isn't the robber."

"So what's his story?" Mr. Cunningham asked as he scribbled notes.

"Mr. Lang says that he was out for an early morning walk," the chief explained. "He says that when he walked by the coin shop, a stranger asked him to help move one of the shop's big cabinets. The stranger claimed to be the new coin shop owner, so Mr. Lang agreed to help. However, the stranger used a pick instead of a key to open the shop's door. Mr. Lang says at that point he became suspicious of the stranger, but he followed him into the shop anyway."

"Not a smart move," said Mr. Cunningham said as he shook his head.

The chief continued, "Mr. Lang says that when they got inside, the stranger saw a light flashing on the security system control panel. The stranger immediately ran for the back door. Mr. Lang says that just as the stranger was going through the back door, the bars came slamming down and they cut the stranger's arm. He says that's why there's blood near the latch."

"Interesting story," Mr. Cunningham said as he scribbled a note. "But my guess is that Mr. Lang was trying to escape when the bars slammed down and cut him. Now he's trying to make up a story so he won't go to jail."

"My thoughts exactly," Chief Riggins agreed. "The security control panel is hidden in the back room. I doubt the thief would have seen a light flashing on the panel and made it out of the store within thirty seconds as Mr.

Lang claims. However, since there isn't a scratch on Mr. Lang, we don't see how it could be his blood," the chief said. "And if he wasn't the one who got cut, maybe there was a different robber after all."

Chief Riggins turned to Dr. Steel. "Dr. Steel, we'd like you to examine Mr. Lang and see if he's hiding a cut somewhere. I have a deputy waiting with him in the back room. Mr. Lang has already agreed to cooperate in the examination because he swears it's not his blood on the latch. But if you find a cut, we'll know he made up this whole story."

Dr. Steel nodded and made his way to the back room.

As Mr. Cunningham asked Chief Riggins a few more questions, Concord wandered over to a chair, dropped his backpack to the ground, and pulled out his Bible. He turned to the concordance section and looked up a few words.

A few minutes later, Dr. Steel came out from the back room.

"Sorry, Chief." Dr. Steel said. "I don't see how that blood can be Mr. Lang's. I searched every millimeter of Mr. Lang and there isn't a scratch or puncture on him anywhere."

Concord leaped up from his chair and pointed to a verse. "There doesn't have to be!" he declared.

"What do you mean?" Dr. Steel asked. Chief Riggins and Mr. Cunningham listened anxiously for Concord's reply.

"I looked up verses about blood and found the answer," The Concordance said. "It's right here in Proverbs 30:33."

CONCORD CUNNINGHAM ON THE CASE: THE *Scripture Sleuth* 3

How could it be Mr. Lang's blood on the door?

Read Proverbs 30:33 for Concord's answer.

The solution to *"Doctors and Detectives"* is on page 92.

6
SAND CITY

Dinner conversation at the Cunningham house was usually lively. But there was one dish that always slowed the conversation to a crawl. Not because the dish was bad. It was because it was so good. No one wanted to stop eating long enough to talk! And tonight Mrs. Cunningham had made that special dish: her famous super-tangy spaghetti.

"I've got it!" cried Concord's older brother, Cody, as the family feasted at the dinner table. "We could build Noah's Ark!"

"Are you expecting a flood?" Concord asked as he shoveled spaghetti into his mouth.

"I don't mean build a real Noah's Ark," Cody explained as he chewed. "I mean build one in the sand sculpture contest at Bigwood Lake this weekend." As he spoke, a drop of sauce shot out of his mouth and landed on his mother's arm.

"Please don't talk with your mouth full, Cody," Mrs. Cunningham said as she wiped her arm with a paper napkin. The rest of the Cunninghams chuckled as they twirled spaghetti in their forks and sucked noodles and sauce into their mouths.

Mr. Cunningham chewed a mouthful and swallowed. "I've never seen anyone try to sculpt Noah's Ark," he said. "If we do a good job, it might just be original enough to get us a prize."

The Cunninghams had entered the sand sculpture

competition every year, but their sculptures had never won any of the many prizes.

"What's this year's theme?" asked Charlotte, Concord's red-haired sister.

"It's called 'Water World'," said Mr. Cunningham. "The rule is that every sculpture must have a pool or channel of water involved in some way. They're putting the sculpture sites right on the edge of the lake so you can just channel the water right into your sculpture."

"Won't the sculptures get washed away when the tide comes in?" asked Charlotte.

Mr. Cunningham shook his head. "There aren't tides on mountain lakes like Bigwood Lake," he said. "Tides come in and out on ocean beaches."

"Noah's Ark would be a perfect sculpture if we're required to have a water feature," Cody said. "We could have water all around the ark like an ocean."

The family nodded in agreement.

"But how does anyone know what Noah's Ark looked like?" asked Charlotte.

Concord swallowed a mouthful. "The Bible tells how wide, long, and tall the ark was in Genesis chapter six," he said. "We could draw a picture using those dimensions, and then that could be our plan for the sculpture."

"That would take a lot of paper to draw the ark using those dimensions," Cody said. "The ark was huge!"

"I think what Concord meant," Mr. Cunningham explained, "is that we can look at the ark's measurements in the Bible and then draw the ark to scale. In other words, we can use the same measurements but on a smaller scale so the drawing will fit on the paper. Our ark will look like a small version of the original. Of course, we don't know exactly what Noah's Ark looked like, but we have a rough idea of its design."

"We'd better start working on it right away," said Cody.

"Right!" said Mr. Cunningham. "I think we have a much better shot at a prize this year with the ark idea than we did last year with the space station."

"Yeah," Charlotte said. "That ended up looking like a burnt down building."

The family laughed as they remembered last year's disaster.

"Of course," Mrs. Cunningham said, "that was because it rained during the last hour of sculpting."

Mr. Cunningham nodded. "This year's organizers are providing canopies over every sand sculpture site," he said. "So if it does rain, all the sculptures should be protected."

"Sounds great!" Cody declared with another mouthful of spaghetti. "Even if it rains we'll be fine." This time, a drop of sauce shot out of his mouth and landed on Mrs. Cunningham's nose.

"It's certainly raining at the dinner table tonight," Mrs. Cunningham said as she wiped her nose. The family howled in laughter, except for Cody, who then heard his mom say, "By the way, Cody, since you talked with your mouthful again, you'll be doing the dishes tonight."

A couple days later, the Cunninghams arrived at the western shore of Bigwood Lake with their buckets, shovels, sculpting tools, and plans for sculpting Noah's Ark. They carried their equipment from the parking lot down to the shoreline, and they found a site under one of the empty canopies.

Concord surveyed the beach and counted twenty-five canopies. The canopies were six feet tall, and they covered about as much space as an average-sized car. The canopies were simply pieces of plastic tarp with four tall poles holding up the corners. They were staked in a row on the edge of the lake.

"Good afternoon, sand sculpture contestants!" a voice boomed from a megaphone. A blond man with a bright yellow tee shirt held the megaphone. He was standing on a fallen log in the middle of the beach.

"Welcome to the annual Bigwood Lake Sand Sculpting Contest," he continued. Everyone clapped. "You will have five hours to create your sand sculpture. The judges will then come around, look at all the sculptures, and decide the winners. Remember this year's rule: all sand sculptures must have water involved in some way. If you create a castle, the water can be your moat. If you create a farm, it can be your pond. Whatever you create must have a water feature."

Then he held a starter's pistol up in the air and said, "On your marks, get set." Bang!

Shovels started digging, sand started flying, and excited contestants started chattering as they began creating their sand sculptures.

"Okay," said Mr. Cunningham, "first let's create the ocean for the ark." All the Cunninghams grabbed their shovels and began digging. They dug a large hole right on the edge of the lake and made sure that one edge of their hole partially opened into the lake. That way, water from the lake would fill the hole.

"It looks like we're making a tiny bay on Bigwood Lake," Cody said.

"Yeah," Concord agreed. "We can call it Cunningham Bay." The family laughed, and Cody gave his little brother a high five.

Cunningham Bay was soon complete, and the family was ready to build the ark. Concord checked his watch. They still had four hours to finish.

After dumping bucket after bucket of sand into the center of Cunningham Bay, they finally had built a mountain of sand for sculpting the ark. They wet the sand, packed it down, and pulled out their sculpting tools.

A few hours later, the ark was nearly finished. Its smooth sides went right down to the water, so it looked like the ark was actually floating.

"How much time do we have left, Concord?" asked Mr. Cunningham as he perfected the trunk of an elephant hanging out one of the ark's windows.

"Twenty-two minutes," Concord replied.

"We're going to finish right on time," Cody said as he carved a bird on top of the ark. "Do you think we're going to win?"

Mr. Cunningham was just about to respond when he heard a thump on top of the canopy.

"What's that?" Mr. Cunningham asked as he continued to carve.

Suddenly, there was another thump. Then another. And another. And then thump after thump after thump.

"It's raining!" Charlotte cried out.

Normally it would be a sand sculpting disaster. But the canopies were protecting the ark and every other sand sculpture on the beach.

"Let's hear it for the canopies!" a contestant down the beach cried out.

"Hooray!" yelled several contestants while others clapped.

The raindrops were splashing into the lake, and Concord smiled as he noticed there seemed to be an invisible line in the water between Bigwood Lake and Cunningham Bay. The lake water was pelted by raindrops, while the water in miniature bay was protected by the canopy.

Then something caught Concord's eye. He noticed that the trees on the shoreline were beginning to bend in the wind. He looked out toward the lake and felt the wind on his face. The wind coming at them was growing stronger.

"Uh-oh," Concord said.

"What is it?" Cody asked.

"It looks like this storm is bringing some strong winds toward our sand sculpture," Concord answered. "That means trouble."

"I don't think so," Cody said. "It would take incredibly strong winds to blow down a sand sculpture. And we can stand around the sculpture so the rain doesn't blow onto it."

Mr. Cunningham had been listening to the conversation. "And," he said, "if you're worried about the canopy, I've already checked it out. It's anchored deep in the ground and all the knots are tight, so it should be fine."

"All of that may be true," Concord said to his father and brother. "But unless we do something, Noah's Ark is going to be ruined."

"What do you mean?" Cody asked.

Concord took two steps across the sand to his backpack and pulled out his Bible. "Read James 1:6," he said. "You'll see what I mean."

Why does Concord think the sand sculpture will be destroyed?

Read James 1:6 to find the clue Concord gave his family.

The solution to *"Sand City"* is on page 93.

7
LENNY THE PEN

Concord loved joining his dad on reporting assignments. He would give up his free time, abandon a fresh plate of chocolate chip cookies, or even miss a good soccer game with his friends if he had the chance to tag along. That is, unless the story was at the local courthouse. Mr. Cunningham's courthouse assignments were usually about long trials that Concord found rather boring.

Today, however, was different. Mr. Cunningham was on his way to the courthouse to report on a local trial, and Concord had begged to join him.

"Do you think they've really found Lenny the Pen?" Concord asked excitedly as they pulled into the courthouse parking lot.

Lenny the Pen was a notorious counterfeiter in the Northwest. He made fake twenty dollar bills, fake driver licenses, fake license plates for bank robbers' getaway cars, and more.

"According to my sources," Mr. Cunningham said, "the person on trial is definitely the man the police suspect. But there really isn't any evidence that he's Lenny the Pen."

"No evidence at all?" Concord asked.

Mr. Cunningham shook his head. "When people get caught using Lenny the Pen's fake goods, many admit that they purchased them from him," he began. "However, Lenny the Pen never meets his customers face to face. He always makes contact through the mail. Because no one has ever seen him, no one can describe him. His packages are always postmarked from a different town, so the police are always one step behind him. And Lenny the Pen is very careful to never leave his fingerprints on any fake item he makes."

"So if there's no evidence, why is he on trial?" Concord asked as they got out of the car. Concord grabbed his backpack off the backseat and closed the door.

"Good question," Mr. Cunningham replied. "The man on trial, Leonard O'Nepper, is actually on trial for stealing his neighbor's car."

"He stole a car from his neighbor?" Concord said with surprise. "That doesn't leave much room for a getaway."

"True," Mr. Cunningham said with a chuckle. "Actually, he was caught driving the car about twenty miles north of Pine Tops after his neighbor reported the car stolen. Apparently, Mr. O'Nepper had the car packed with suitcases and belongings, which suggests he was going away for good."

"Just like Lenny the Pen would always go from one town to another to stay ahead of the police," Concord added.

"Right," agreed Mr. Cunningham. "Anyway, Mr. O'Nepper says he didn't steal the car. He claims that his neighbor actually sold the car to him. But his neighbor says that's a lie. This is the trial to figure it all out."

The Cunninghams entered the courthouse and went straight to the courtroom. It was packed. Fortunately, Mr. Cunningham's press pass allowed the Cunninghams to cram their way onto a press bench near the front of the room.

"Which table is for the defendant?" Concord asked. He knew that Leonard O'Nepper was the defendant in this case because he was accused of the crime.

Mr. Cunningham pointed to a table on the right side of the courtroom. Sitting next to his lawyer was a tall, middle-aged man wearing thick glasses. "That must be him," Mr. Cunningham said as he began scribbling notes in his notebook. There were no cameras allowed in the Pine Tops courtroom, so Mr. Cunningham wrote down as many descriptive notes as he could.

"All rise!" the bailiff suddenly barked from the left side of the courtroom. The judge entered the courtroom from a side door and took his seat.

"Please be seated," the judge said as he shuffled through papers on his desk. The judge was an older man with large cheeks and gray hair combed straight back.

Over the next hour, the lawyers established all of the major facts. Mr. O'Nepper's neighbor, Mr. Hill, owned a flashy new sports car. Mr. Hill always parked it on the street in front of his house. Mr. Hill looked out his window one morning and saw that his car was gone. He immediately called the police and reported the car stolen. About an hour later, the police pulled over Mr. O'Nepper who was driving the car on a highway north of Pine Tops.

Concord was just starting to lose interest in the trial when the crowd suddenly started to mumble. Concord scanned the courtroom and realized that Mr. O'Nepper was walking up to the witness stand to testify.

"Mr. O'Nepper," his lawyer said, "let's see if we can clear up a few things."

"Gladly," Mr. O'Nepper said.

"You've been accused of stealing your neighbor's car, but that's not true, is it?" his lawyer asked.

"Not at all," Mr. O'Nepper said. "Here's what happened. Mr. Hill and I were talking one afternoon. I mentioned that the weather forecasters said it may snow that night. Mr. Hill couldn't believe me because it was the first weekend in June. It hasn't snowed in June in Pine Tops since the 1800s."

"What happened next?" his lawyer asked.

"I assured Mr. Hill that the forecast called for snow," Mr. O'Nepper said. "He laughed at me and said that if it snowed, he would give me his new car."

Returning to his table, the lawyer picked up something and turned to the judge. "Your honor," he said, "Here is a newspaper from the day after that conversation. It clearly shows that it did snow that night." He approached the judge and handed him the newspaper.

"I remember the storm," the judge grumbled in a gruff voice.

The lawyer turned back to Mr. O'Nepper. "So, you took the car because you thought it was yours," the lawyer said.

"That's right," agreed Mr. O'Nepper. "Mr. Hill made a bet and I won."

The lawyer nodded and began walking back to his table. He stopped halfway there and turned back toward Mr. O'Nepper. "I have one more question for you. Are you Lenny the Pen?"

The courtroom was absolutely silent as everyone waited for the response.

"Absolutely not!" Mr. O'Nepper declared. "I don't know how anyone could even think such a thing. If there's any evidence out there, I'd sure like to see it."

The lawyer smiled at Mr. O'Nepper. "Thank you, Mr. O'Nepper," he said. Mr. O'Nepper stepped down and returned to the defendant's table. "Your honor," the lawyer said, "I'd like to call one more witness to the stand: Mr. Hill."

Mr. Hill rose from his seat and walked up to the

witness stand. He was a short man with a mustache and red hair.

"Mr. Hill," the lawyer began, "do you remember the conversation that Mr. O'Nepper just described?"

"I don't," Mr. Hill said with a laugh. "You don't think I'd really tell somebody that I'd give them my car if it snowed, do you?"

"Mr. O'Nepper says that you did," the lawyer said. "He says that you made a bet. You were betting that it wouldn't snow. If you lost the bet, you'd give Mr. O'Nepper your car. And that's exactly what happened. Now Mr. Hill, you are a man of honor aren't you?"

The smile disappeared from Mr. Hill's face. "Of course I am," he said.

"Then shouldn't you honor this bet you made with Mr. O'Nepper," the lawyer said. "If you don't, not only will you lose your honor for not following through with your word, but you might just send an innocent man to jail. I can't think of anything more dishonorable than that."

Mr. Hill's brow tightened in confusion. Then he shook his head. "Look," he said, "you're twisting this whole thing around. I never told Mr. O'Nepper that I'd give him my car if it snowed."

"How do we know that?" the lawyer asked.

"I guess it's my word against his," Mr. Hill said.

Concord and the rest of the courtroom continued listening to Mr. Hill as the lawyer asked him a few more questions. But Mr. Cunningham, with his reporter instincts, kept a close eye on Mr. O'Nepper at the defendant's table.

A few moments later, Concord leaned over to his dad. "It looks like there's no way we're going to find out what really happened, huh Dad?" he whispered. Mr. Cunningham didn't respond. "Dad?"

"What?" Mr. Cunningham whispered. "Sorry, Concord. I've been watching Mr. O'Nepper. A moment ago, he took a piece of paper off the stack on his table." Concord scanned the defendant's table and saw a stack of fresh paper in a tray on the corner of the table.

"Is that paper there so the defendant can take notes?" Concord asked.

"Right," Mr. Cunningham replied. "But Mr. O'Nepper doesn't seem to be listening to the questions. I think he's working on something else."

Concord gasped quietly. "Do you think that Lenny the Pen is in action?" he asked.

Mr. Cunningham was about to answer when Mr. O'Nepper called his lawyer over to him. Mr. O'Nepper whispered in his lawyer's ear for a minute and then handed him a sheet of paper.

"Is that the paper he's been working on?" Concord asked.

"Yes," Mr. Cunningham said as he stretched his neck to see better. "I haven't taken my eyes off of him. After he carefully took the sheet off the stack, he slid it across the table to a spot in front of himself. He wrote on it for a few moments and then carefully slid it off the table and handed it to his lawyer."

The lawyer walked over to Mr. Hill. "Mr. Hill," the lawyer said, "I have in my hand a note written by you. Would you read this aloud please?"

Mr. Hill looked at the paper and then looked back at the lawyer. "I don't understand," Mr. Hill said. "I don't remember writing this."

"It is your handwriting, isn't it?" the lawyer asked with a smirk.

"Well, yeah but—"

"Please read it aloud," the lawyer insisted.

Mr. Hill swallowed hard and then read, "Hey Leonard, it looks like it snowed after all. Be nice to my car. Signed, Rob Hill."

"Is that your signature?" the lawyer asked.

"Well, yeah, but I really don't remember writing this," Mr. Hill said. "I've written funny little notes to Mr. O'Nepper in the past, but I never wrote this."

"Mr. O'Nepper just told me that he found this letter in an envelope in his mailbox the day after the snow," the lawyer said. "Obviously, you were lying when you said you never told Mr. O'Nepper that you'd give him your car if it snowed. So, Mr. Hill, it looks like your car really does belong to Mr. O'Nepper."

As the courtroom crowd began to buzz with surprise at the turn of events, Concord turned to his dad. "Who should we tell about what you saw?" Concord asked.

Mr. Cunningham rubbed his chin. "I'm not sure," he said. "Mr. Hill already said that letter was in his own handwriting. Even he couldn't tell that it was a fake! If I interrupt the trial to accuse Mr. O'Nepper of forging that letter and no one can tell that it's a fake, I could be in big trouble."

"But if somebody can tell that it's a fake, it would prove that Mr. O'Nepper is trying to cheat," Concord said.

"And it also would prove that Leonard O'Nepper is Lenny the Pen," Mr. Cunningham whispered excitedly. "No one could forge a letter in somebody else's handwriting on the spot except Lenny the Pen."

Concord put his hand to his forehead. "Wait a minute!" he whispered excitedly. He quickly reached for his backpack and pulled out his Bible. He flipped through the pages for a minute and then tapped on a verse. "Yes!" he said. "Dad, you'd better get the judge's attention. We've got a way to catch Lenny the Pen."

"Do you mean that you can tell if the letter is a fake?" Mr. Cunningham asked. "Some police experts can't even tell when they're looking at Lenny the Pen's fake writing."

"This time it's not the writing that we need to look at," The Concordance said. "It's the paper. I think it may be just like Ephesians 5:27, but it shouldn't be."

How will Concord prove that the letter is a fake?

Read Ephesians 5:27 for the clue that Concord gave his dad.

The solution to *"Lenny the Pen"* is on page 94.

8
THE
SUPERDRINK

It had been a while since the Burley twins were last seen at their favorite bench by the school cafeteria. The muscular, blond twins loved to jump onto the bench and try to trick students out of their lunch money before it was spent on lunch.

However, a few months ago Principal Ironsides started his lunchtime patrols, and the Burley twins were out of business. Principal Ironsides kept a close eye on the bench and on the twins. Whenever he saw the twins doing something suspicious, he would hurry over to inspect.

It definitely slowed down the trickery of the Burley twins, but it didn't quite stop it. The Burley twins knew that one day, sooner or later, even Principal Ironsides would get sick and miss a day of school. That day finally came.

"Step right up, everybody!" Bart Burley called from the bench in front of the cafeteria. Concord and his friend Charlie Lowman, along with everyone else, had just been dismissed from class for lunch.

"Uh-oh," Charlie said. His messy hair bounced slightly as he walked. "The twins are at it again. Who's going to stop them with Mr. Ironsides gone?"

"The truth will," Concord said as he tapped his backpack. Charlie smiled, knowing that Concord's Bible was always in his backpack.

Concord and Charlie worked their way toward the front of the crowd. A moment later, Bart waved his hands up and down to quiet everyone. Then he pointed to his brother, Bernie, who was doing jumping jacks a few feet to the right of the bench.

"Welcome, friends!" Bart cried out to the crowd. "My brother Bernie and I have made an amazing discovery, and we'd like to share it with you."

"Jumping jacks have already been discovered," somebody called out. The crowd chuckled at the joke.

Bart chuckled, too, and then continued. "We're not here to show you how to do jumping jacks," he explained. "We're here to tell you how you can have the energy to do ten times the jumping jacks you can normally do!"

Students looked at the twins with curiosity.

"Check out my brother," Bart continued. "He must be doing fifty jumping jacks each minute!"

Charlie leaned over to Concord. "He really is doing jumping jacks like crazy," Charlie whispered. "I wonder what this secret energy of theirs is?"

"Don't forget that the Burley twins are great athletes," Concord cautioned. "Bernie might have trained himself to do fast jumping jacks."

Bart continued his speech. "Friends," he said to the crowd, "you may be wondering how my brother could get so much energy. Just imagine what you could do with that kind of energy. You could do homework ten times faster. Or you could score more points in sports. Or you could have more energy to help your parents around the house and maybe get some extra allowance. I know what you must be asking yourselves: How can I get this energy?" Bart reached down into a paper bag and pulled out a glass jar. It was filled with a chunky yellow and orange mixture. "Here's the answer," Bart called out. "This is the Burley Twins' Superdrink!"

The crowd buzzed with interest.

"That's right," Bart said. "The Superdrink can give you super energy!" He held the jar up to his mouth and began drinking and chewing the chunks. A few moments later the jar was completely empty, and Bart let out a satisfied sigh. "I feel better already!" he boasted. "While I work off some of this energy, Bernie will tell you more." Bart set the empty jar on the bench and began doing jumping jacks.

Bernie stopped doing his jumping jacks and picked up the empty jar. "The Superdrink is a special formula that we invented," Bernie said.

"How did you invent it?" Charlie asked.

"Good question," Bernie replied. "We wanted to find a nutritious drink that would boost our energy, so we started experimenting with different mixtures. After weeks and weeks of trying, we finally found a mixture that gave us super energy. And that's why we call it the Superdrink."

Concord began to wonder if there was anything dangerous in the drink. "Would you be willing to tell us what's in the Superdrink?" he asked.

"I see that even Concord Cunningham is interested in the Superdrink," Bernie said with a smile to the crowd. "I'll bet that he could flip through the pages of his concordance ten times faster with the Superdrink!" Then Bernie realized that everyone was waiting to hear the answer to Concord's question. "Oh yes, the ingredients to the Superdrink. I'm sure that everyone will be glad to know that the Superdrink is made from only healthy ingredients that you can find in any kitchen."

The crowd nodded in approval as Bernie explained. "The ingredients of the Superdrink are lemon juice, bread crumbs, salt, one peach, and honey. They're all natural, and I'm sure you all have them in your cupboards at home."

"So now that we know the ingredients, I guess we can all go make Superdrinks of our own," Charlie said.

"Not quite," Bernie replied. "The key to the Superdrink is getting the exact amount of each ingredient. You see, it took us hundreds of tries to get all the amounts exactly right. If just one of the ingredient amounts is slightly off, the drink won't work."

"Why not?" a student asked.

"Because of the way the Superdrink ingredients react to each other," Bernie explained. "When just one of the amounts is slightly off, the reaction won't be correct and you won't get super energy." Bernie smiled as he held up a large stack of paper. "That's why we printed everything you need to know on these sheets. Each sheet tells you the exact amounts of the ingredients and exactly how to make the Superdrink. And even though it took us weeks and weeks to come up with the exact formula, we're selling each instruction sheet for the very low price of three dollars."

Charlie watched a couple students reach into their pockets. "It looks like a few people think that's a pretty good deal," he said. He scratched his head as he thought. "I guess you could make as many Superdrinks as you wanted to if you had the instructions."

Before Concord could reply, Bernie continued with his sales pitch. "My brother and I also decided to do something unusual. We're going to tell you exactly what's on the instruction sheet. That way, you'll know just how easy this is."

Charlie leaned over to Concord. "Why do you think they're doing that?"

"Probably so people will trust them a little bit more," Concord answered. "Besides, I doubt anybody will be able to write everything down as quickly as they say it.

So, they don't have to worry about their recipe being stolen. At least until they sell it."

"Yeah," Charlie said, "but by then they'll have everybody's money anyway."

Bernie continued, "The instructions tell you that you need one teaspoon of lemon juice, one-fourth of a cup of wheat bread crumbs, one-half of a teaspoon of salt, one whole peach weighing exactly seven ounces, and one-third of a teaspoon of honey.

"When you have all of the ingredients," Bernie continued, "here are the mixing instructions." He looked down at the sheet and read. "Put all the ingredients in a large drinking glass or a jar and mix them together with a fork. Make sure you don't use a blender. That could mix the drink too much and the Superdrink reaction might start in the blender instead of in your stomach. When you use the fork, you'll have to squash the whole peach pretty good. But do not cut the peach or puncture the peach's skin in any way before it is in the glass or jar. Some juices might escape and then the peach will have a different weight. After the peach is squashed and you're done mixing the Superdrink, drink it and enjoy your super energy!"

Concord stepped forward to ask Bernie a question. Charlie stepped forward, too, and stood by Concord's side. "When did you mix up the Superdrink that Bart just drank?" Concord asked.

"I'm glad you asked!" Bernie replied. "We did it right here a few minutes ago. That's the great thing about the Superdrink. You can take it anywhere and fix it when you need it. Just measure out the ingredients and bring them along in separate containers. Then mix them together when you're ready. If you're getting ready for a big test, mix up a Superdrink! If you're about to run a race, mix up a Superdrink! Or if you're about to chop some wood, what should you do?"

Bernie held his hand up to his ear and leaned toward the crowd. The crowd chanted, "Mix up a Superdrink!" Everyone started to applaud, except Concord. He had another question.

"You said that the peach weighs exactly seven ounces," Concord said. "Isn't it hard to find a peach that's exactly seven ounces?"

Bernie nodded. "You might think so," he replied. "But there are so many peaches at the grocery store. All you have to do is keep weighing peaches on the grocery store scale until you find one that weighs exactly seven ounces. Remember, after you find one, don't cut it open until you're squashing it into the drink with your fork. Otherwise, some of the peach juice might escape and the peach's weight will change. As I said, if you use a peach that weighs more or less than exactly seven ounces, you'll have the wrong amount of peach in your stomach. Then you won't get the Superdrink reaction."

Bernie put Bart's empty Superdrink jar on the bench so he could begin selling instruction sheets. Concord studied the jar for a moment. Then he reached into his backpack and pulled out his Bible.

Bart, who was still doing jumping jacks, saw Concord with his Bible. He immediately stopped his jumping jacks and hurried over to Concord.

"What are you doing?" Bart whispered nervously. "I thought we answered all of your questions."

"You did," Concord said with a grin. Then he looked up from his opened Bible. "Now I have a question for you about the Superdrink that you drank a couple minutes ago." Concord picked up Bart's jar and turned it upside down to confirm that it was empty. "You and your brother claim that when you make the Superdrink the instructions must be followed exactly."

"That's right," Bart agreed.

"Did you follow the Superdrink instructions when you made this one?" Concord asked as he held up the jar. Then he set it back on the bench. "Or, are you ready to admit that this whole thing is just a scam."

Bart stood still, trying to decide what to say. Then he looked over at Bernie who was selling the Superdrink instructions to a long line of students. He turned back to Concord. "I followed the instructions, of course," he said as he nervously cleared his throat.

"I think you and I both know that's not true," Concord said. Then he held out his Bible and pointed to a verse. Bart leaned over and read it. He thought for a moment, and then his cheeks turned red.

"What is it Concord?" Charlie asked. "How did you know?"

"It's something in Genesis 1:11," The Concordance replied. "If they really did follow the instructions, Bart couldn't have finished that drink."

How did Concord know that Bart couldn't have finished the drink if he followed the instructions?

Read Genesis 1:11 for the clue that Concord gave Charlie.

The solution to *"The Superdrink"* is on page 95.

9
A FISHY FIASCO

"It looks like we've got two choices," Mrs. Cunningham said to her family. The Cunninghams were just about finished with a fun day at the state fair. "There's a pig judging contest going on in the main barn, or there's a fireman competition in the arena."

"I'd vote for the fireman competition," Mr. Cunningham replied.

"My nose agrees with you, Dad," Concord said, remembering how bad the fair barn had smelled the last time he was in there.

"And my shoe agrees with you, too, Dad," Cody said, remembering the manure he had stepped in the last time he was in the fair barn.

Mrs. Cunningham and Charlotte weren't very fond of pigs, either. So a few minutes later, the Cunninghams were seeking seats in the arena to watch the fireman competition. They were lucky to find three seats in the front row with two more seats directly behind them. Mr. Cunningham and the boys sat in the front row, and Mrs. Cunningham and Charlotte sat in the two seats in the second row.

"Ladies and gentleman," the arena speakers blared as the Cunninghams settled into their seats, "it's now time for the spray-o-war!"

The audience roared. Concord raised an eyebrow. "What's a spray-o-war?" he asked his dad.

Mr. Cunningham pointed to a long cable running above the arena floor. It stretched across the arena just like a tightrope. Hanging down from the cable in the middle of the arena was a large metal ball. "When that metal ball gets pushed, it slides on the cable," Mr. Cunningham explained. "So the firemen divide into two teams and each team tries to push the ball to the other team's end of the cable. It's like a tug of war, except they're pushing instead of pulling."

"How do they reach all the way up there?" Concord asked.

"They don't," Mr. Cunningham replied. "They spray the ball with their fire hoses."

"Cool!" Concord exclaimed.

A few moments later, a whistle blew and the spray-o-war began. Both teams were very accurate with their spraying, and the ball was staying within a few feet of the center of the arena. Slowly, one team began to make progress, and the metal ball worked its way toward one end of the cable. Then, when the metal ball was just a few feet from the end, one person on the winning team stepped on a teammate's foot. That teammate began to stumble and stepped on another teammate's foot. Suddenly, the whole team had tripped and fallen to the ground. The aim of their hose swung away from the metal ball and into the audience!

"Watch out!" Mr. Cunningham cried. But it was too late. The water shot straight into Concord, Cody, and Mr. Cunningham, and they were absolutely drenched. Mrs. Cunningham, Charlotte, and the rest of the audience roared in laughter.

The water stream had only hit the boys and Mr. Cunningham for a couple seconds, but it was enough to completely soak their shirts and hair.

"Well," Mr. Cunningham said as he wiped his wet hair off of his forehead, "maybe we should have chosen the pigs."

Since they didn't have any spare clothes, the family decided it was time to head home. A couple minutes later, they were near the fairgrounds exit when a voice caught their attention.

"Step right up!" a man called out from a colorful booth. "Three ping pong balls for only one dollar!" The Cunninghams stopped to look in the booth. Inside was a large table holding hundreds of plastic cups, with a goldfish swimming inside each cup.

The carnival worker noticed that the Cunninghams were looking at the fish. "Hi folks!" he said. He saw that Mr. Cunningham and the boys were wearing wet shirts. "Was there a rainstorm around here that I didn't hear about?"

"Only if you were at the fireman competition," Concord said.

"So were you boys on fire?" the worker joked. He continued talking before they could answer. "Well, let me help make your day a little bit brighter. For one dollar you can have three ping pong balls to throw at these cups. If one ping pong ball lands in a cup, you win the cup and the fish that's inside it!"

"Sounds easy enough," Mr. Cunningham replied. He turned to the kids. "Anybody want a fish?"

Concord and Cody shook their heads.

But Charlotte cried, "I do! I do! I've always wanted my own goldfish!"

Mr. Cunningham looked at his wife, who shrugged with a smile. "Why not," she said. "As long as you promise to take good care of it, Charlotte."

"I will," Charlotte replied. "I promise!"

"Well, then," Mr. Cunningham said as he pulled out his wallet. "Let's see how lucky you are."

Mr. Cunningham handed a soggy dollar bill to the carnival worker, who then handed three ping pong balls to Charlotte.

"Good luck," the carnival worker said.

Charlotte squinted as she studied all the goldfish cups. She noticed that the prettiest fish were near the edge of the table. She shook a ping pong ball in her hand, aimed for a pretty fish, and threw the ball. It bounced from one cup rim to another, and then bounced off the table. Charlotte moaned.

"That's okay, Charlotte," Mr. Cunningham said. "Try again."

She threw a second ball and the same thing happened.

"Hey, Charlotte," Concord said. He leaned over and whispered in her ear. "Try throwing your ball as close to the middle of the table as you can. That way it has more chances to bounce into a cup."

She whispered back, "But those fish in the middle aren't as pretty."

Concord replied, "Isn't a fish that isn't pretty better than no fish at all?"

She shrugged and decided to take Concord's advice. She took a deep breath and lofted the ball to the middle of the table. It bounced off one cup rim, then another, and another, and even another. Finally, after six bounces, it landed in a cup!

"We have a winner!" the carnival worker shouted.

"Yes!" Charlotte shouted. The Cunninghams all clapped and whistled.

The carnival worker plucked out the ball, picked up the cup, and handed it to Charlotte. "Congratulations," he said. "Take good care of your fish."

"I will!" Charlotte said with a smile. She looked down at the fish. It was dull orange and fairly small. It wasn't nearly as pretty as the fish in the cups on the edge of the table, but she was still glad to have it.

The Cunninghams thanked the man and walked out the fairgrounds exit.

"Now comes my least favorite part of the day," Cody said, "the walk back to the car."

"Yeah," Concord agreed. "I think we're parked in the next county."

"Just about," Mr. Cunningham replied. "Maybe one of these days the fairgrounds will get a bigger parking lot."

"It's only about a fifteen minute walk to the car," Mrs. Cunningham said. "It'll be good exercise."

They trudged along the shoulder of the road. Concord was in front of everyone, trying to set a good pace. After seven or eight minutes, Concord heard a scream. It was Charlotte!

"Ahh!" she cried. "Oh no!"

Concord spun around and saw Charlotte lying in the weeds on the shoulder of the road. She had tripped and dropped the fish cup when she fell. It had landed upside down in the weeds, and all of the water had run out of the cup.

"My fish!" she cried. "Help!"

Cody rushed over and gently scooped the fish back into the empty cup.

"He's going to die without water in his cup," Charlotte said as tears welled up in her eyes.

"Anybody see a creek nearby?" asked Mr. Cunningham. Concord scanned the landscape, but saw only trees and bushes.

"What if we run back to the fairgrounds and get some water?" Cody asked.

"He won't live that long!" Charlotte cried. "Look, he's already starting to wiggle slower."

Concord looked at the fish and knew that Charlotte was correct. The fish was struggling and wouldn't survive much longer.

Mr. Cunningham began to fear the worst. "It's okay, Charlotte," he assured her. "It was an accident. We can always go back and win another fish."

Concord's eyes opened wide. "Wait!" he exclaimed. "We can save this fish!"

"How?" Charlotte asked. "He's only got a minute or two of life left."

"That's all we need!" Concord said.

"What are you talking about, Concord?" Mrs. Cunningham asked. The rest of the family waited for Concord's response.

"Judges 6:38," The Concordance replied. "I know it'll work!"

How will Concord save the fish?

Read Judges 6:38 for Concord's clue.

The solution to *"A Fishy Fiasco"* is on page 96.

10
THE
INTERNATIONAL
BALLOON BURGLAR

Quite a few things fell out of the sky in Pine Tops. Along with the usual rain, snow and hail, Pine Tops residents also had to watch out for falling pine cones. The slightest breeze could knock several cones out of any of the town's large trees. Though the pine cones weren't that heavy, they could sting worse than a bee if they fell fifty feet and hit you on the head.

There were also pine needle blizzards. Many of the old needles on the pine trees would cling to the branches until a strong wind blew, and then they would all let go at the same time. Cars could be covered in minutes if they were sitting under the right group of trees on a windy day.

But perhaps the most exciting thing to ever fall out of the sky came one evening just before the Cunningham family sat down for dinner.

"Dad, look!" Concord yelled as he pointed out the kitchen window. Mr. Cunningham looked up from the sink where he was washing his hands and gazed out the window. His hands suddenly stopped scrubbing. There, floating down from the sky, was a skydiver! The skydiver's red and white parachute was open, and he was drifting toward the east side of town.

"Oh my!" Mr. Cunningham said. "Who could that be?" He quickly rinsed his hands and dried them on a towel next to the sink. Then he turned to Concord. "Let's go!" he said excitedly.

Concord was thrilled that he didn't need to ask if he could come along. As Mr. Cunningham grabbed his reporter's notebook and cell phone, Concord slung his backpack over his shoulder.

A moment later they were in the car. "Do you see him?" Mr. Cunningham asked excitedly.

"He's coming down right over there!" Concord exclaimed as he pointed to the left.

"It looks like he's headed for White Bark Hill," Mr. Cunningham said. "Of all of the places in Pine Tops, that's probably a pretty good choice."

"Why's that?" Concord asked as he leaned forward to look through the windshield.

"It's one of the few places in town without thick groves of trees," Mr. Cunningham explained. "There's actually some open land to hit." Mr. Cunningham flipped on the car's blinker and took a sharp left onto White Bark Hill Road.

"He's landing!" Concord exclaimed as they drove up the curvy road. A few seconds later the skydiver was yanking the parachute's steering ropes and guiding himself to a landing. Then, as he touched the ground with medium speed, he did a shoulder roll to break his fall.

"Nice landing," Mr. Cunningham said to Concord. "This guy's a pro."

As the skydiver began collecting his chute on the ground next to White Bark Hill Road, the Cunninghams arrived alongside him in their car.

Mr. Cunningham rolled down the window. He immediately noticed a badge on the skydiver's arm. Concord also noticed the badge and asked, "Do you think he's with the FBI or CIA?"

"I'm not sure," Mr. Cunningham said. "I don't recognize the design of the badge. Let's see if we can get a little information."

Mr. Cunningham opened his reporter's notebook in his lap and stuck his head out the window. "Nice landing, sir," Mr. Cunningham said.

The skydiver walked over to the car and took off his helmet. Mr. Cunningham immediately blushed with embarrassment when he saw the skydiver's long brown hair and lipstick. The skydiver wasn't a he, but a she!

"I'm Francine Renault with the Canadian Police," she said as she held out her hand. "Nice to meet you."

"Likewise," Mr. Cunningham said as he shook her hand. "I'm Bill Cunningham, and this is my son, Concord." Concord and Officer Renault nodded at each other. "So what brings you to Pine Tops?" Mr. Cunningham asked.

"The balloon burglar," Officer Renault replied.

"There's a burglar in Canada who steals balloons?" Mr. Cunningham asked as he scribbled a note on his notepad.

Officer Renault chuckled. "Not quite," she said. "He uses balloons to sneak away the money he steals."

Mr. Cunningham paused and looked up. "How does he do that?" he asked.

Officer Renault continued collecting her chute as she explained. "The balloon burglar finds the business he wants to rob and tries to get hired there," she said. "He makes sure he gets a job where he has access to the cash register. After a couple of months, he secretly takes all the money out of the cash register and sneaks to either a back door or a roof. He puts the money in a bag and ties it to a big bunch of helium balloons. Then he lets them go and goes back to work. A few minutes later he claims that the store got robbed."

Mr. Cunningham rubbed his chin. "He doesn't have the money on him, so there's no evidence that he's the one who took it."

"Right," Officer Renault said. "And he always works in a place where there isn't a security camera, so no one can see that it was he who took the money out of the cash register."

Concord leaned over to ask Officer Renault a question. "How does he get the money back if it's floating away with the balloons?"

"Good question, young man," Officer Renault replied. "That's what we just figured out. The balloon burglar also puts a small transmitter in the money bag. It sends out a location signal which allows him to track the balloons. We finally locked onto the signal from one of his thefts and tracked the signal here."

"To Pine Tops?" Mr. Cunningham said with surprise. "That's hundreds of miles!"

"The balloon burglar had some bad luck," Officer Renault replied. "Right after he launched his balloons, a storm front passed through. The strong winds caught the balloons and they've apparently been traveling at high speeds for a couple of days. That's how they made it so far."

"Do you think the balloon burglar is still coming for his money?" Mr. Cunningham asked.

"No," Officer Renault replied. "He was captured at the border. We finally got one step ahead of him. However, the money is still missing. And this was his biggest robbery yet. He was working at a large sporting goods store and took one thousand dollars from the cash register at the end of the day."

"Just out of curiosity," Mr. Cunningham asked, "why did you come here by parachute instead of by car?"

"We had no idea where the money would land," Officer Renault explained as she finished collecting her chute. "It could have been somewhere without any roads. We also knew that we needed to get to it before anyone else. We decided that this would be the best way to get to it fast."

She pulled a device out of her pocket and flipped one of its switches. It started beeping. Mr. Cunningham was just about to ask about the device when Concord tapped him on the arm.

"Dad, look," Concord said, "it's Chief Riggins."

Chief Riggins' patrol car came to an abrupt stop next to the Cunningham car, and the chief quickly hopped out. He hurried over to Officer Renault. "Officer Renault, I'm Chief Riggins" he said as he held out his hand. "It's nice to meet you face to face."

"Thanks for coming so quickly," Officer Renault said. "I know I only gave you short notice when I radioed from the airplane."

"No problem," the chief said. He turned towards the Cunningham car. "I see that you've met our local reporter and our local Concordance," he said as he winked at Concord.

"Concordance?" Officer Renault repeated. Before she could ask the chief to explain, she heard another beep from her device. "We'd better hurry," she said.

Chief Riggins followed Officer Renault up the road. Concord and Mr. Cunningham hopped out of their car and followed a few steps behind. The device began beeping quicker as they neared a house.

Officer Renault stopped and pointed at the house. "The money's in there," she said.

Chief Riggins nodded. "That's Jerry Elmore's house," he said. "Follow me."

The group walked up the sidewalk towards the door. Concord and his dad stopped a few feet before the porch and let Chief Riggins and Officer Renault approach the door. The chief rang the doorbell. A moment later, Mr.

Elmore opened the door. He was a short man without much hair, and he wore a white turtleneck and a green plaid vest. His face went pale when he saw Chief Riggins and Officer Renault.

"Hello," Mr. Elmore said cautiously.

"Hello, Mr. Elmore," Chief Riggins said. He motioned to his left. "This is Officer Renault, who has tracked something to your house. Did you happen to find a bunch of balloons with a bag attached to it?"

Mr. Elmore gulped. "I did," he said. "Wait right here." Mr. Elmore went back into his house.

A moment later, he returned. He was holding a large bunch of balloons tied to a brown leather bag. "The balloons got tangled in a tree in my yard last night at about seven o'clock," Mr. Elmore said. "I pulled them and the bag down." He handed the balloons and bag to Chief Riggins, who handed it to Officer Renault. She ripped a patch off the side of the bag and pulled the transmitter out of the lining. She held it up for everyone to see.

Then Officer Renault opened the bag. "What?" she exclaimed. "It's empty! Where's the money?"

Everyone looked at Mr. Elmore. He gulped again. "Well," Mr. Elmore said nervously, "I spent it."

"You spent it?" Officer Renault replied. "Didn't you think it might belong to somebody else?"

"I figured that whoever sent it into the sky was trying to get rid of it," Mr. Elmore said. "I mean, who would send money away like that if they wanted to keep it?" He scratched his head. "I guess if I would have known about that transmitter hidden in the bag, maybe I would have called the police. But I didn't know it was there."

Chief Riggins and Officer Renault weren't sure if Mr. Elmore had broken any laws, so they didn't know what to do. But Concord was beginning to have an idea.

"Could I ask a question?" Concord asked the two officers.

Chief Riggins nodded. Officer Renault was confused. She wasn't sure why the chief would let a boy get involved in the investigation.

Concord stepped forward. "Mr. Elmore, where did you spend the money?" he asked.

"I did something that I've always wanted to do," Mr. Elmore replied with a smile. "I drove over to the homeless shelter in Bigwood City, and I invited nineteen homeless people to dinner with me at the nicest restaurant in town."

"The Golden Grizzly?" Chief Riggins asked.

"That's right," Mr. Elmore replied. "Not only that, but I bought each person a Fifty Dollar Feast. Everyone was thrilled."

"What's a Fifty Dollar Feast?" Officer Renault asked.

"It's a special deal at the Golden Grizzly," Chief Riggins explained. "You pay fifty dollars, and you get a fancy steak dinner, gourmet appetizers, a deluxe salad, a huge dessert, and a bottomless beverage. Tax and the tip are also included, so you spend an even fifty dollars."

Mr. Cunningham did some calculations on his notebook. "So, including yourself," Mr. Cunningham said to Mr. Elmore, "you bought twenty of the Fifty Dollar Feasts. That equals exactly one thousand dollars."

"Right," Mr. Elmore said. "I spent exactly the amount of money in the balloon bag. Not a penny more or less. So, unfortunately, every penny of the money is gone."

Officer Renault sighed. She knew that the money would be difficult to get back if it had already been spent at a restaurant. Then she noticed that Concord was running to his car. A moment later he came running back with a Bible in hand.

"Chief Riggins," Officer Renault said, "what exactly did you mean when you said that this boy was the local Concordance?"

Chief Riggins looked at Concord, who was flipping through his Bible pages. "I think you're about to find out," the chief said.

A few seconds later, Concord looked up at Officer Renault. He stared at the Canadian Police badge on her arm for a moment. Then he looked back at a verse in his Bible and nodded. "Chief, I think you'd better get a warrant to search Mr. Elmore's house."

"What for?" the chief asked.

"I don't think Mr. Elmore's story is true," Concord replied.

"You don't?" Officer Renault said with surprise. "Why not?"

"It can't be," The Concordance said. "There's a clue right here in Matthew 22:19-20."

How did Concord know that Mr. Elmore was lying?

Read Matthew 22:19-20 for the clue that Concord gave Officer Renault and Chief Riggins.

The solution to *"The International Balloon Burglar"* is on page 97.

11
PEANUT
BUTTER POWER

"Is it true that you can use a potato instead of a battery to run a digital clock?" Charlie Lowman asked Concord. The two friends were entering the Pine Tops Youth Center.

"It's true," Concord replied as he held the door open for Charlie. "I saw a demonstration on a science show once. The scientist connected a potato to a small digital clock. He used wires, paperclips, and pennies. The clock actually started running!"

"So if a clock can run on a whole potato, does that mean my watch could run on a potato chip?" Charlie asked.

The boys chuckled. "Maybe we'll find out today," Concord replied as the youth center doors shut behind them. Concord darted into the nearby coatroom and hung his backpack on a hook. A moment later he was back with Charlie, and the two boys surveyed the surroundings.

The youth center was hosting this year's alternative power contest. It was sponsored by the local power company, Northwest Power. Kids from all over the area brought their ideas for different ways to generate electricity. There were drawings, displays, and all sort of models set up in rows of booths. The winner of the contest would receive a $1,000 savings bond. The boys began a slow walk through the aisles of ideas. A few minutes later, a short man jumped onto a small stage at the end of the room.

"Good afternoon ladies and gentlemen," the man said. He wore a white shirt and a yellow tie. "I'm Joe

Stockman, the coordinator of today's competition. Thank you all for coming. The judges have looked at all the ideas here today and have narrowed the contest down to two finalists. We'd like each of the two finalists to make a short presentation up here on the stage before the judges make their final decision."

Everyone in the room was silent as Mr. Stockman looked down at his clipboard to read the names of the two finalists.

"And the two finalists are Rachel Jackson from Bigwood City," Mr. Stockman said with a pause while everyone applauded, "and Holly Chan from Pine Tops." Again everyone applauded.

"Alright!" Charlie said with a grin and a nod. "There's a local kid in the finals." Concord nodded with Charlie and clapped.

After a few minutes, the two finalists had set up their displays on the stage and were ready to make presentations. Everyone in the youth center gathered around the stage to watch.

Mr. Stockman stepped up to the microphone again. "Our first finalist presentation will be by Rachel Jackson from Bigwood City," he said. He moved off the stage, and the audience politely applauded for Rachel.

Rachel was a short girl wearing a red sweatshirt, a green baseball cap, and glasses. She had set up a model of a windmill with a shiny black base. She pointed to the windmill with a long stick and said, "My idea is to combine two old ways of generating electricity into one new one. I call it the solar mill. The top of the unit is a windmill and the bottom is covered with solar panels. This way, no matter what the weather, the solar mill will be generating electricity. If it's sunny, the solar panels will generate power. If it's stormy, the windmill will generate power. And if it's both sunny and windy, it will generate twice the power."

"That's pretty good," Concord said to Charlie.

"Yeah," Charlie agreed. "As long as it's not cloudy and calm."

A few moments later, Rachel was done with her presentation. She left the stage while the judges scribbled notes on their pads and considered her idea.

Mr. Stockman jumped back onto the stage. "Our other finalist is Holly Chan from Pine Tops," he said. Again, the audience politely applauded. Holly was a thin girl wearing a white tee shirt and a pony tail. She stepped up to the front of the stage and pointed to a cake plate with a tall lid.

"Ladies and gentlemen," Holly began, "my idea is a simple one. So simple, and yet so surprising, that you'll hardly believe it." People in the audience looked at each other in curiosity. "No doubt you've heard about potatoes and sometimes lemons being used as batteries to power clocks," she continued. Concord and Charlie nodded at each other and exchanged a high five. "But there's something else that can power clocks that no one has ever discovered. Until now." She dramatically ripped the lid off the plate. On the plate were wires, paperclips, pennies, a running clock, and something surprising: a sandwich.

"Is that her idea or just her lunch?" Charlie joked.

"This is no joke," Holly assured the audience. "This is the world's first peanut butter battery."

The judges scratched their heads as the audience laughed in disbelief. Concord and Charlie decided to make their way to the front edge of the stage to get a closer look. When they got there, they saw two slices of white bread with a triple thick layer of peanut butter in the middle.

Charlie's stomach suddenly growled. He put his hand on his stomach and explained, "I haven't eaten lunch yet."

"Yeah, it actually looks pretty tasty," Concord agreed. "Except for those wires."

The sandwich had a black wire and a red wire inserted into the middle of it. The sandwich was inside a clear sandwich bag that had been sealed shut with tape. Outside of the bag, the wires wrapped around pennies and paper clips and then attached to a digital clock. The clock seemed to be running perfectly.

"One day," Holly explained. "I wondered if peanut butter could be used as a battery in the same way as a potato or lemon. At first it didn't work. But then I tried wiring a peanut butter sandwich and sealing it in a sandwich bag." She pointed to the tape which sealed the bag. "For some reason, that made the difference and the clock started to run."

Charlie nudged Concord. "Do you think this is for real, Concord?" he asked.

"I'm not sure," Concord replied. "I never really understood how the potato battery worked."

Charlie looked over at the judges who were whispering to each other as they considered the peanut butter battery. "It looks like the judges aren't sure either," Charlie said.

"There are many advantages to this new power source," Holly continued. "For example, you've all seen the expiration dates on peanut butter jars. Think about what happens to all the peanut butter that expires in cupboards and on store shelves. Now, instead of people and stores just throwing their old peanut butter away, they could use it for power. In fact, that's why my mom let me try this experiment. We had a jar of expired peanut butter that she was going to throw away. I would have been in trouble if I'd used the good stuff."

The parents in the audience chuckled.

"Finally," Holly said, "there's one more reason that peanut butter is a great new power source. It lasts for months! Think about it. Even if your peanut butter is a year old, it still looks the same. A potato or lemon battery won't last nearly that long."

Holly then pointed to the clock at the end of the wires.

"To illustrate this point, I used a stopwatch with this peanut butter battery."

Concord took a closer look at the clock and realized that the clock was, in fact, operating in stopwatch mode.

"I started this stopwatch when I first connected the peanut butter battery. If you take a close look, you'll see that it's been running exactly one month, one week, two days, four hours, three minutes, and six seconds."

The audience gasped. The judges quickly rose from their chairs and walked over to the peanut butter battery. The first judge who inspected the clock nodded in agreement with Holly. Then he turned to her and asked a question. "So you haven't touched this peanut butter battery since you started the stopwatch?" he asked.

"Nope," Holly said proudly. "That bag has been sealed since the first minute. I hope when you decide who wins today's contest, you remember how truly amazing this discovery is."

While the audience burst into applause, Concord suddenly had an idea. He hurried out of the crowd and went back to the coatroom where his backpack hung on a hook. Charlie followed, though he couldn't keep up with Concord's quick moves. When Charlie finally caught up, Concord had his Bible out and was pointing to a verse.

"I thought so," Concord said. "Something just wasn't right about Holly's display. Now I know what it is."

"Do you mean that the peanut butter battery is fake?" Charlie asked. "How do you know?"

"It's right here in Joshua 9:12," the Concordance replied. "It's something that she forgot to consider when she made up her story."

How did Concord know that Holly's story about the peanut butter battery was a lie?

Read Joshua 9:12 for the clue that Concord gave Charlie.

The solution to *"Peanut Butter Power"* is on page 98.

12
THE GREATEST CASE

"Concord!" Charlotte yelled as she ran toward the soccer field. "Come quick! You're not going to believe this!" She had run all the way from downtown Pine Tops to Evergreen Park where Concord was playing soccer with his friends.

Concord froze and looked across the field at Charlotte. She started jumping up and down and waving for him to come with her.

Concord kicked the soccer ball to his friends one last time and began running to Charlotte. He was so curious about what she wanted that he forgot to pick up his backpack. Halfway to Charlotte he realized his mistake and ran back for the pack. After he grabbed it, he quickly turned around and ran toward Charlotte again. A few moments later he was standing next to his sister and gasping for air.

"What happened?" Concord asked as he tried to catch his breath. "Is there a mystery that somebody wants me to solve?"

"It's already been solved!" Charlotte said excitedly. "There's another Scripture Sleuth in Pine Tops!"

Concord's jaw dropped. He could hardly believe it. He knew that there were others who were trying to solve mysteries with their Bibles. A few had even asked him for tips. But until now, no one else had actually done it. As the news sunk in, Concord's stunned expression changed into a huge smile. He loved the idea of somebody else being able to use the Bible to solve mysteries!

"Who solved the mystery?" Concord asked.

"Paul Peterson," Charlotte said. "He's at the camera shop downtown. That's where it just happened. I thought you'd want to know, so I ran straight here."

"Thanks," Concord said with a nod. "Let's go!" Concord took off for the camera shop and Charlotte hurried alongside him. A block before they arrived, Concord began to get curious. "So what happened in the camera shop?" he asked.

"Mom and I were in the shop getting some film," Charlotte explained. "There was a customer there who was trying to return a telescope. He said that the telescope wasn't working because he couldn't find a distant star that he was looking for. Paul Peterson was in the shop, too, and he overheard the customer talking to the salesman. Paul mentioned a Bible verse that says something about the east and the west. The customer suddenly realized that he had been looking in the wrong direction for his star. The problem was solved!"

"Terrific!" Concord replied as they approached the camera shop. Charlotte suddenly stopped and pointed. "There's Paul on the bench in front of the shop," she said. Paul was a chubby boy with thick brown hair. He was about Concord's age, and he wore a striped shirt and baggy blue jeans.

Concord thanked Charlotte, who then ran off to meet Mrs. Cunningham at the nearby ice cream shop. Concord walked over to Paul and introduced himself. "Hi Paul, I'm Concord," he said as he held out his hand. "Congratulations for solving your first case as a Scripture Sleuth!"

Paul shook Concord's hand and smiled. "Thanks, Concord," he replied. "I've been hearing about you for a long time. I've always wanted to solve a mystery like you.

I think I just got lucky this time, though," he said with a shrug.

"Why do you say that?" Concord asked.

"Well, I've tried to solve mysteries before, and this is the first time I've actually been able to do it," he said. "I'm not sure if I'll be able to do it again, but I'll keep trying." Paul lifted his Bible off the bench and flipped through the pages. "The Bible sure is loaded with good stuff for solving mysteries. I'm glad that whoever wrote the Bible made it such a long book."

"God wrote the Bible," Concord replied. He sat down next to Paul.

"What do you mean?" Paul asked.

Concord dropped his backpack to the ground and pulled out his own Bible. He flipped to the book of 2 Timothy. "It says in 2 Timothy 3:16 that all Scripture is given by inspiration of God," he said as he pointed to the verse. "That means that when the Bible was written, there were people holding the pens but God gave them the words to write."

"I didn't know that," Paul replied. He thought for a moment. "It must be the best book ever written!"

Concord smiled. "It's got my vote," he agreed. "God's Word is perfect. Unfortunately, we're not."

"What do you mean?" Paul asked.

"Well, I'm sure you've heard the saying 'nobody's perfect'," Concord began.

"Yep, and it's true," Paul said with a nod. "I'm living proof of that."

"I am, too," Concord replied. They chuckled at themselves, and then Concord continued. "Nobody is perfect because we all make mistakes. And we all choose to do the wrong thing at one time or another. In other words, we all sin. In fact, the Bible says in

Romans 3:23 that all have sinned and fall short of the glory of God."

Concord flipped the pages of his Bible to Romans to show Paul the verse. Paul leaned over and read it. Then he rubbed his chin. "I've always heard that sinning was bad. But if everybody in the whole world sins, what's the big deal?" Paul asked.

"The big deal is that God is perfect," Concord explained, "so there can be no sin in His presence, including in heaven."

"Wait a minute," Paul said. His forehead wrinkled with concern. "Does that mean that I can't go to heaven because I'm not perfect?"

"Well, there's good news and bad news about that," Concord replied. "First, here's the bad news." He flipped forward a couple pages. "The Bible says in Romans 6:23 that the wages of sin is death. In other words, Paul, you're right. Since you haven't lived your life perfectly, just like everybody else, you don't deserve to be in heaven when you die." Concord looked over at Paul, who had a frown on his face. "But here's the good news. That same verse then says that the gift of God is eternal life in Christ Jesus our Lord."

Paul rubbed his forehead in confusion. "Does that mean there is a way to heaven after all?"

"Yes, and much more," Concord began. "It also means that you can have a new life in Jesus right now. You can live for God instead of living for yourself and for sin. But the Bible makes it clear that there's only one way to get to heaven and to have a life with God. It's through Jesus." Concord quickly flipped his Bible pages over to the book of John. "As Jesus says about Himself in John 14:6, He is the way and the truth and the life. No one comes to God except through Him."

"Why is Jesus the only way?" asked Paul.

"That's a good question," Concord said. "To get the answer, you need to know who Jesus is. He is God's Son. He is eternal. It says in John 1:1 that He was with God in the beginning and He is God. When Jesus was born into the world, He was born of a virgin. Jesus wasn't born with a sinful nature like everybody else because God is His Father. Jesus is the only one who's ever lived His entire life without sinning. Even so, He was nailed to a cross and killed."

Paul was stunned. "What? Why was He killed so horribly if He never did anything wrong?" he asked.

"Because God sent Jesus to take the penalty for your sin," Concord answered. "Dying on the cross is the price that you and I and everyone else should have paid for all of our sins." Concord paused for a moment to let it all sink in. Paul swallowed hard as he thought about what Jesus did. Then Concord continued. "After Jesus died on the cross, He was buried in a tomb. But, on the third day He rose from the dead! Now He sits at the right hand of God the Father."

Paul was beginning to understand what Jesus had done. "So, because Jesus died in my place, I can be forgiven for all of my sins?" he asked.

"That's right," Concord replied with a smile.

"Whew," Paul said with relief. "So am I a Christian now that I know all of that?"

"Not quite," Concord answered. He bit his lower lip as he tried to figure out a way to explain. "You see, it's not enough to just know the facts."

"What do you mean?" asked Paul.

"A true Christian is someone who has received Jesus as Savior and Lord in his or her heart." Concord flipped pages again and quickly found the verse he was looking for. "It says in John 1:12 that to all who receive Jesus and believe in His name, He gives the right to become children of God. That means that if you receive Jesus as your Savior and Lord you'll be forgiven, you'll have a relationship with God, and Jesus will be in charge of your life."

Paul looked at the verse in Concord's Bible. "So how do I receive Jesus?" Paul asked.

Concord looked up at Paul. "You pray," he answered gently. "You admit to God that you are a sinner and that only Jesus can save you. You tell God that you're willing to turn away from sin and submit to Him. And then you ask Him to save you and ask Jesus to come into your heart as your Savior and Lord. And He will. He guarantees it. The Bible says in Romans 10:13 that everyone who calls on the name of the Lord will be saved."

Paul stared down at the bench for a moment as he thought. Then he looked up at Concord. "I think I'm ready to receive Jesus as my Savior and Lord," he said. Then Paul rubbed his chin. "But first, I have one more question. Even though we're all sinners, God never gave up on us. He even sent His own Son to die for us. Why?"

Concord nodded and then grinned. "For that," The Concordance said, "you might want to check out John 3:16. And then, if you're ready, we can pray."

Read John 3:16 for Concord's answer to Paul's question.

The solution to *"The Greatest Case"* is on page 99.

Solutions

Solution to The Lost Lumberjack

John 13:5 describes how Jesus washed his disciples feet. Concord realized that Mr. and Mrs. Gilliam's feet also should have been "washed." They claimed they were swimming in the lake when they saw the statue. They also said that after they saw it they climbed into their boat and went straight to McCall's dock. However, when Concord first saw them, both of them had sandy feet. If their story about finding the statue was true, their feet would have been washed off while they were swimming in the lake.

Upon further questioning, Chief Riggins discovered that the Gilliams had stolen the statue themselves and towed it to the eastern shore of the lake. They then claimed to "find" it so they could receive the reward money.

A few hours later, the couple was in jail, the statue was returned to the town square, and Pine Tops birds had their favorite perch back.

Solution to Pine Tea

Proverbs 26:20 says that when there is no wood the fire goes out. Concord realized that if both Rusty and Lefty had fallen asleep after their first cup of tea (as Lefty had claimed), no one would have been awake to keep the fire going. The fire would have burned itself down or out long before all the tea could have steamed away.

Lefty confessed that he drank all the tea and promised to find another Schwandt Pine to make Rusty the tea he owed him. It didn't take long. Lefty found a Schwandt Pine growing near the Cunningham house and brewed a pot of tea in the Cunninghams' kitchen.

The two riders decided to share their kettle of tea with the Cunninghams, who thought the tea tasted strangely similar to the secret ingredient in Mrs. Cunningham's lemonade.

Solution to The Face Scribbler

James 1:23 refers to a person seeing himself in the mirror. Concord realized that John had no way of seeing his own reflection while he was out at the big boulder. Therefore, he shouldn't have known that there was ink on his face.

John said that when he woke up he discovered that somebody had drawn on his face. However, no one else was there to tell him he had ink on his face. John claimed that he was asleep during the entire scribbling, so he wouldn't have felt someone drawing on his face. He also claimed that he had brought nothing with him when he went out to the big boulder, so he couldn't have seen his reflection in anything. Finally, Concord's inspection of John's hands showed that no ink had rubbed off his face onto his hands. So, he couldn't have discovered the ink by seeing it on his hands after touching his face.

Caught in his lies, John admitted that he had written on his own face in an attempt to get Robbie into trouble. Principal Ironsides was about to give John cleaning duty as punishment, but he changed his mind at the last minute. Instead, he ordered John to not wash the ink off of his face for the rest of the school day.

Solution to Redhead Roses

1 Corinthians 3:6 refers to Paul planting something and Apollos watering it. Concord realized that if the Redhead Rose bushes were sealed inside a box for two months and only received fresh air, they wouldn't receive any water. It would only be a matter of time before they would wilt or die due to a lack of water, and they certainly wouldn't be producing flowers.

When told of the design flaw, Mr. Oliver immediately stopped selling the Redhead Rose Machine, and KONE-FM was back to regular programming within a matter of minutes.

The next spring, the Pine Tops Flower Shop introduced the Redhead Rose Machine II. This time, it had a water line.

Solution to Doctors and Detectives

Proverbs 30:33 refers to the "wringing of the nose" producing blood. Concord realized that Mr. Lang could have given himself a nosebleed to get the blood on the door latch. Afterwards, he could have stopped the bleeding and wiped his face. He would have produced the blood without putting a scratch on his body.

Mr. Lang didn't confess after Chief Riggins confronted him with the explanation. However, Mr. Lang later decided to admit to the crime when the shop's owner arrived and revealed a secret security video camera which had recorded the whole event.

Solution to Sand City

James 1:6 refers to waves of the sea being blown and tossed by the wind. Concord realized that the storm's winds would be whipping up waves on Bigwood Lake. Because the sand sculpture was created in Cunningham Bay, a miniature bay of the lake, the waves would splash right into the bay and hit the ark. Unless something was done, the sand sculpture would be washed away in no time.

Fortunately, because of Concord's quick thinking, the Cunninghams had time to build a big wall of sand to protect the ark from the waves. The Cunninghams also ran up and down the shore warning the other contestants about the coming waves. All but two of the sand sculptures were saved.

Once again, the Cunninghams didn't win a prize for their sand sculpture. However, they did receive a special award for helping other contestants save their sculptures.

Solution to Lenny the Pen

Ephesians 5:27 refers to not having a wrinkle or any blemish. Concord realized that the forged letter would be in perfect condition. Mr. Cunningham said that Mr. O'Nepper had carefully pulled the piece of paper from the stack of fresh paper on his table, written on it, and then carefully slid it off the table and handed it to his lawyer. However, Mr. O'Nepper claimed that the letter had been put in an envelope and placed in his mailbox. If this was true, the letter would have been folded and the paper would have creases.

Mr. Cunningham decided to take a chance and speak out. Just before the judge threw him out of the courtroom for disrupting the trial, he saw Concord with an open Bible in the next seat. The judge decided to examine the letter and discovered that it did not have creases from being in an envelope as it should have.

It was declared a fake, and Lenny the Pen was finally caught.

Solution to The Superdrink

Genesis 1:11 refers to trees in the land that bear fruit with seeds. Concord knew that the Superdrink instructions called for a whole peach to be put in the Superdrink. Since the directions said that the peach shouldn't be cut open before putting it in the drink, it would still have a peach pit in the middle. Bart could not have swallowed or chewed up a hard peach pit as he drank his Superdrink, yet his jar was empty.

Furthermore, even if the recipe for the Superdrink was real (which it wasn't), it would mean that the drinker would always have to eat the peach pit in order to get all seven ounces of peach in his or her stomach. And almost no one would be willing or able to do that.

The twins didn't admit to the crowd that the Superdrink was a fake. However, they quickly refunded everyone's money after claiming that they had just realized that there were side effects from the drink (such as lying and confusion).

Principal Ironsides was back at school the next day and students once again went to lunch in peace, except for the strange sounds their stomachs made after eating cafeteria food.

Solution to A Fishy Fiasco

Judges 6:38 refers to wringing water out of a fleece. Concord realized that he, Cody, and Mr. Cunningham could wring (or squeeze) the water out of their wet shirts into the fish cup.

Sure enough, the three of them squeezed their shirts and it nearly filled the cup. The fish survived, and Charlotte decided to name it "Lucky."

Solution to The International Balloon Burglar

Matthew 22:19-20 refers to the image and inscription on a piece of money. It helped Concord remember that the stolen dollars were from a store in Canada, so they would be Canadian dollars.

Some American businesses near the Canadian border do accept Canadian dollars. However, Canadian dollars and United States dollars are not equal in value. Even if the Golden Grizzly did accept Canadian dollars, the one thousand stolen Canadian dollars would not be the correct amount to exactly pay the one thousand dollar restaurant bill. Since Mr. Elmore claimed it had worked out exactly right, Concord knew he was lying.

Officer Renault stayed with Mr. Elmore while Chief Riggins got a search warrant. Upon the chief's return, the house was searched and the money was found. After falsely claiming to eat a fancy meal the night before, Mr. Elmore was now stuck with the jailhouse dinner tray.

Solution to Peanut Butter Power

Joshua 9:12 refers to bread becoming moldy (or, in the NASB, "crumbled"). Concord realized that if the sandwich had been sealed in the bag for more than a month as Holly (and the stopwatch) claimed, the bread would have become moldy. However, when Concord and Charlie had examined the sandwich, they thought it actually looked quite tasty. So, Concord knew that the sandwich could not be anywhere near a month old.

After Concord presented the evidence to the judges, they opened the sandwich bag and discovered a battery hidden in the thick layer of peanut butter. Holly then admitted that she had made up everything and was disqualified.

Solution to The Greatest Case

John 3:16 says that God so loved the world that He gave His only begotten Son. It was because of God's great love for you that He sent Jesus to save you. If you have not yet received Jesus as your Savior, are you ready to do so right now?

Here's the prayer that Paul prayed with Concord. You can pray it, too, and receive Jesus as your Savior and Lord. But remember, just saying these words isn't the key to being saved. God is listening to what's coming from your heart.

"God, I confess that I am a sinner. I'm sorry for all the wrong things that I've done. Please forgive me for all my sins. I believe that Jesus died on the cross for my sins, that He rose from the dead, and that I can only be saved through Him. I receive Jesus as my Savior and Lord and ask Him to come into my heart. Jesus, please be Lord of every part of my life. Thank you. Amen."

If you have prayed a prayer like the one above, you are now a Christian. This means that you have a personal relationship with Jesus Christ! To grow in your relationship, remember to read the Bible daily, pray often, obey God, and find a church that honors Jesus Christ and preaches the Bible as the perfect and complete word of God.

Concord's Secret

If your Bible has a Concordance, it will usually be found at the back of the book. It is a collection of the most common words found in the Bible, with their most used examples in the text under the word. Sometimes there is a brief description of what the word means. Learning how to use a Concordance gives a Bible scholar a marvelous tool for finding God's Truth on any subject in His Holy Word.

Below are a few examples of words found in the Concordance. Read them for practice, look up the verses, and you will see how much fun it is to do your own Scripture Sleuthing. Then get your Bible and you will be able to solve your own mysteries in life.

Appearance - brightness, radiance, sight
I Samuel 16:7, man looks at the outward *appearance*
Matthew 6:16, for they neglect their *appearance*
Matthew 28:3, his *appearance* was like lightning

Friend -
Proverbs 17:17, a *friend* loves at all times
Proverbs 18:24, a *friend* who sticks closer than a brother
John 15:13, lay down his life for his *friend(s)*

Impossible -
Matthew 19:26, with men this is *impossible*
Luke 1:37, nothing will be *impossible* with God

Money - gain
Ecclesiastes 5:10, who loves *money* will not be satisfied
Mark 6:8, no *money* in their belt
I Timothy 3:3, free from the love of *money*
Luke 19:23, why ....not put the *money*.....bank

Parents -
  Matthew 10:21, children will rise up against *parents*
  Romans 1:30, disobedient to *parents*
  Ephesians 6:1, children, obey your *parents*

Sword -
  Genesis 3:24, flaming *sword* which turned
  Psalm 57:4, their tongue, a sharp *sword*
  Ephesians 6:17, the *sword* of the spirit
  Proverbs 5:4, sharp as a two-edged *sword*

Glad -
  Matthew 5:12, rejoice and be *glad*
  Proverbs 10:1, wise son makes a father *glad*
  2 Corinthians 11:19, bear with the foolish *gladly*

Serpent -
  Genesis 3:1, Now the *serpent* was more crafty
  Psalm 58:4, venom of a *serpent*
  John 3:14, Moses lifted up the *serpent* in the wilderness.
  Matthew 10:16, be shrewd as *serpents*

Trouble - distress, affliction
  I Kings 20:7, see how this man is looking for *trouble*
  Job 5:6, does *trouble* sprout from the ground?
  Psalm 9:9, a stronghold in times of *trouble*
  Proverbs 10:10, who winks the eye causes *trouble*

If you have enjoyed solving the mysteries along with Concord Cunningham, you may wish to read

Concord Cunningham:
The Scripture Sleuth
ISBN 1-885904-19-3

The Scripture Sleuth 2:
Concord Cunningham Returns
ISBN 1-885904-25-8

The Scripture Sleuth 3:
Concord Cunningham On The Case
ISBN 1-885904-39-8

The Scripture Sleuth 4:
Concord Cunningham Coast to Coast
ISBN 1-885904-53-3

Visit the Scripture Sleuth website at
www.scripturesleuth.com

For other biblical titles from Focus Publishing visit
www.focuspublishing.com